THE GASPARDS OF PINE CROFT

RALPH CONNOR

This Book was given to me by Alice Nov. 27 1925 in anticipation of my birthday tomorrow

Will J. Clapp

By RALPH CONNOR

THE GASPARDS OF PINE CROFT

TO HIM THAT HATH

THE SKY PILOT IN NO MAN'S LAND

THE MAJOR

THE PATROL OF THE SUN DANCE TRAIL

CORPORAL CAMERON

THE FOREIGNER

BLACK ROCK

THE SKY PILOT

THE PROSPECTOR

THE DOCTOR

THE MAN FROM GLENGARRY

GLENGARRY SCHOOL DAYS

THE GASPARDS
OF PINE CROFT

A ROMANCE OF THE WINDERMERE

Gordon, Charles William, 1860-

by

RALPH CONNOR pseud.

NEW YORK
GEORGE H. DORAN COMPANY

COPYRIGHT, 1923,
BY GEORGE H. DORAN COMPANY

THE GASPARDS OF PINE CROFT. I

———

PRINTED IN THE UNITED STATES OF AMERICA

THE GASPARDS OF PINE CROFT

THE GASPARDS OF PINE CROFT

CHAPTER I

Of all British Columbia valleys none has a finer sweep than the spacious Windermere. The valley rolls itself on both sides of the Columbia River in wide stretches of grass lands, varied with great reaches of red pine forest, here of open park-like appearance, there thick with underbrush of spruce and cedar. The valley lies between the two ranges of the Selkirks, which in places crowd hard upon the river and again lie up against a far horizon across a stretch of tumbling foothills. With the autumn sun on its rich and varied wealth of color, the valley lies like one great genial smile across the face of British Columbia from Golden Pass to the Crow's Nest, warm, kindly, restful.

It was upon a glorious autumn day that Hugh Gaspard's eyes first rested upon the valley, and from that first impression he could never escape. For, though by training and profession Gaspard was an engineer, and with a mastery of his craft, by native gifts of imagination and temperament and sense of colour, that rarest of Heaven's bestowments, drawn from his mingled Highland Scot and Gallic blood strain, he was an artist.

Gaspard was enormously proud of this mingled blood of his. He was never quite sure which strain brought him greater pride. It depended entirely upon his en-

7

vironment. In Glasgow, where his father's engineering works were situated and where he spent his boyhood, he was never tired vaunting the "Gaspard" in his blood. In Paris, where in early youth he spent his holidays and where later his hard-headed and practical father declared he "wasted two valuable years of his life fiddlin' wi' pents and idle loons and lassies," he was vehemently Highland, a cousin, indeed, to the Lochiel himself. From both strains he drew his fiery, passionate, imaginative temperament, his incapacity, too, for the hard grind in life.

After graduating from the Glasgow University as an engineer, his father reluctantly granted him a period of travel, upon condition that he should visit Canada and study the engineering achievements in the construction of the Canadian Pacific Railway through the Rocky Mountains. His experiences in the construction of that great continental railroad, together with his holiday excursions among the mountains and valleys of British Columbia, determined for him his course in life. The prospect of life in an office in Glasgow, no matter how high the position, nor how rich in financial possibilities, became for him utterly impossible.

"Let me work among the machines and the men— I've learned to handle men a bit in Canada—and I'll make a stab at it," he had said to his father. But his father was at the end of his forbearance with him.

"Ye've ta'en ye're ain gait," the old autocrat had flung at him, dropping into wrathful Doric, "these many years. Now ye'll go whaur ye're bid in my business or ye'll go oot."

So "oot" the young man had gone, and in the Construction Department of the Canadian Pacific Railway had found a billet at once remunerative and promising of distinction in his profession. After a couple of years of really strenuous work, for he had found himself brigaded with a group of keen youngsters ambitious of distinction and voracious of hard work, with whom his pride would not suffer him to break step, he returned home, loaded down with trophies of his hunting trips and with his portfolio full of incomplete sketches of marvellous mountain scenery. But he had with him also equally marvellous photographic reproductions of the achievements of the Canadian Pacific Engineers, and a bank book showing a very creditable balance in the Vancouver Branch of the Bank of Montreal. The really fine display of heads of Rocky Mountain sheep and goats and the quite creditable productions of his sketch book had but the slightest influence with his father; but the photographs, in themselves wonderful examples of artistic work, the engineering triumphs they pictured, and, it must be confessed, the showing of the bank book most of all, produced a profound impression upon the shrewd old Scot.

The glories of the Windermere Valley, its vast agricultural and grazing resources, its immense water powers, its unknown mineral resources, its unequalled climate, and the unique opportunity offering at the very moment for the purchase of a five thousand acre tract of land from the Government at a quite ridiculous price, lost nothing in their setting forth by the descriptive powers of his son, backed up as they were by gorgeously coloured literature issued by the Immigration Department of British Columbia. Only one result could follow. His father, swept completely beyond the moorings of his life-long shrewd and calculating "canniness" by his son's glowing presentation of the opportunity not only of winning for himself a very substantial fortune but also of becoming that thing dear to every British heart, a great landed proprietor, frankly surrendered, and, having surrendered, proceeded to follow up his surrender in a thoroughgoing business-like manner. If a ranch were to be started in British Columbia, let it be started in such style as to insure success. None knew better than the old Scot how easily possible it is to kill a thoroughly sound enterprise by early starvation. Hence, there was placed in the Bank of Montreal, Vancouver, a sufficient sum, not only to purchase the land, but also to adequately, even generously, equip and stock the ranch.

The two years spent in building, equipping and stocking operations in connection with the establishing of the Pine Croft Ranch constituted for many years the high-water mark for princely expenditure in British Columbia, which is saying a good deal. For many months the Golden-Crow's Nest trail was periodically choked with caravans of pack ponies and freight wagons piled high with a weird assortment of building material and equipment and household furnishing, later enlivened with lines of thoroughbred Holsteins and Percherons. The Windermere Valley was thrilled with the magnificence of the whole enterprise. The Vancouver *Free Press* chronicled the event in laudatory terms:

"The establishing of the Pine Croft Ranch upon such an assured foundation is at once a testimony to the far-sighted policy of our enterprising and gifted fellow-citizen, Hugh Gaspard, Esq., and an evidence that a new era has dawned for our Province. The capitalists of the homeland have hitherto been blind to the unrivalled agricultural and ranching possibilities of our wide-sweeping British Columbia valleys. Mr. Gaspard is very shrewdly anticipating the advent of an almost limitless market for the products of his ranch by the construction of another great railroad through the mountains, with lateral colonisation lines to the main line of the Canadian Pacific Railway. It is also no small tribute to the engineering genius of Mr. Gaspard that he has foreseen the vast resources of the Windermere Valley in water power for mining operations which are sure to follow the railway development of that part of the Province. Altogether, it is not too much to say that the establishing of the Pine Croft Ranch inaugurates a new era in the development of our Province."

The Pine Croft Ranch was situated about halfway down the Windermere Valley, between Golden and the

Crow's Nest Pass, in one of the mighty loops of the Columbia River, and comprised within its bounds mountain and valley, lake and stream, grass lands and park-like forests, a wonderland of picturesque and varied beauty.

For the site of his ranch bungalow, Gaspard chose one of the park-like forest benches of the Columbia, set out with tall red pines with polished boles running up one hundred and fifty feet to spreading green tufts. It was built of red pine logs, with low roof and wide verandahs, and flanked on one side with gardens, riotous with flowers of all kinds and colours, some gathered from their native wilds near by and others transplanted from their native haunts in Scottish glens and moors. On the other side of the bungalow ran a little river, tumbling noisily and joyously from the upper branches of the Columbia River below. It offered to the eye a satisfying picture of homely beauty, kindly, cosy, welcoming. Beyond the riot of flowers a grass paddock of some five acres reached to the corals and stables.

Within the bungalow everything in furnishing and adornment suggested comfort and refinement. In the living room the walls of polished pine logs were hung with old tapestries, the rich red brown of the logs relieved by the gleam of old silver from diamond-paned cupboards and bits of old china and Oriental jade, with a rare collection of ancient pewters disposed here and there. The note of easy comfort in the room was emphasised by the Persian and Assyrian rugs, with the skins of grizzly and cinnamon bear upon the floor, together with the solid, deep-seated chairs and sofas upholstered in leather. Altogether, it was a wholly livable room, in which everything in the way of furnishing and adornment spoke of sound and educated taste. Opposite the main door, a stone built fireplace of generous size gave promise of cheer throughout long winter evenings. On each side of the fireplace a door led to dining room and kitchen respectively, while through a curtained archway on the

left a corridor ran, flanked on either side with bedrooms.
On the remaining side of the living room, folding
doors opened upon a sunny room looking toward the
north and west, enclosed on three sides with panelled
glass. This room, from its appointments and furnish-
ings, obviously did double duty as studio and work
room.

To this home in the British Columbia wilds, far from
the homeland and friends of the homeland, remote from
the great world and its allurements, he brought as his
wife the daughter of a West Country laird. A young
girl she was, fresh from her English school, the first fine
bloom of her girlhood still upon her, the sweet purity of
her soul unspoiled by the defiling touch of our modern
society, her high spirit unbroken, her faith in man and in
God as yet unshaken.

The manner of his coming upon her was of a piece
with the romantic passion within which his spirit en-
shrined her. Upon one of his tramps along the West
Coast he found himself on an evening in a driving fog,
hopelessly lost and with the prospect of a dreary night
in some cheerless wind-swept cave. Out of the mist,
sprite-like, she came, her blue eyes looking in upon his
soul from an aureole of misty golden curls, and led him,
her captive on the moment and forever after, to her home.
That evening was the beginning and the end for them
both. He talked and she listened. She sang and he
played. Of the Windermere and its wonders he told her,
drawing the very soul out of her till, by the sweet pain
in her heart, she knew that when he said the word she
would follow him to the world's end. And to the Windermere he brought her, proud of her beauty and her grace,
wondering at her love of him and praising God for his
good fortune.

Ten years they lived there together, ten happy years
untouched by grief, but for the day when they laid up on
the hillside under the pines her little girl, her very replica
in exquisiteness of beauty. Then shadows came. Her

strength began to fail and though her high courage kept the truth from her husband the knowledge of it grew in the hearts of them both and shadowed their lives with a nameless fear of what might be.

CHAPTER II

"And what's 'fore-ornained,' Mother?" The hazel grey eyes searched the face, pale and luminous as if with an inner light, leaning toward him. "What's 'fore-ornained?'"

"'Fore-ordained,' darling? Why, it means—well, let me see—why, well—it's a little hard to explain, darling."

"I'm glad it is, Mother, because I don't want to be stupid. I'm glad you don't know either."

"Oh, well, I don't quite say that, Paul, but it is a little difficult. You see it is difficult to explain about God."

"Oh, no! Not difficult about God. Why! I know God just as well as—anything."

"Do you, dear?"

"Yes, and I often see Him——"

"See Him, darling?" The mother's voice was a little shocked. "What *do* you mean? When do you see Him?"

"Oh, lots of times. But mostly when I lie down on my back under the big pine trees away up on the hill here, Mother, and look away up between the big tops into the clouds—no, I mean behind the clouds—way up through the little blue holes—I see Him looking down at me, quiet, quiet, oh, awful quiet—just like He was watching and thinking—you know, just like you sometimes when you look far, far away over the river and away far behind the mountains, at something you don't see. That's the way He looks down through the clouds and between the trees, and He sees me too but He never says anything out loud—just looks and looks, and whispers—just like little winds."

"And what does He look like, darling? I mean what —who does He make you think of?" asked the mother.

14

"Oh, I don't know azackly. Oh, yes, a'course—why, I never thought before, Mother—it's you, a'course. Only He's a man an' bigger—oh, much bigger, and stronger." The little boy paused a moment or two, then said shyly, "An' I like Him, Mother, awful well."

"Do you, darling? And why?"

"Oh, I dunno. He's always nice and pleased looking. An' I think He likes me. But, Mother, you didn't answer me about that word 'fore-ornained.' "

" 'Fore-ordained?' Well, let me see—what does it say? 'The decrees of God are His eternal purpose, according to the counsel of His will, whereby for His own glory He hath fore-ordained whatsoever comes to pass.' Well, that just means, Paul, that God has arranged beforehand everything that happens in the world."

"Everything? To everybody? Every single thing?"

"Yes. Yes, dear. Now, we'll go on."

"But everything, Mother? To Blazes too?" insisted the boy, his eye upon the nondescript mongrel stretched at ease on the grass in the shade of the verandah.

"To Blazes? Why—I suppose so—yes."

"Are you sure, Mother, about Blazes?" said the boy, with a child's passion for absolutism.

"Yes, of course—but now let us get on." The mother, from long experience, feared a pitfall.

"God didn't arrange about Blazes' ear. It was the big wildcat did that when Blazes sailed into 'im. Daddy said so," said the boy triumphantly marshalling his secondary causes in the great line of causation. "I guess God doesn't arrange for dogs, does He, Mother?"

"Why—yes, dear."

"But are you sure, Mother, certain sure? Sure as death?" insisted the boy.

" 'Sure as death?' Where did you get that, Paul?"

"Oh, that's what Jinny says, only she says, 'sheer as deeth,' " said the little lad, proud of the superiority of his diction over that of his old Scottish nurse. "Are you sure, Mother, about Blazes?" he persisted.

"Yes, dear, I am sure. You see, Blazes had to learn that it's dangerous to 'sail into' wolves—or a wildcat, was it?—and so——"

"And so God arranged the wildcat for to teach him. My, that was awful clever of God. And God arranged for the wildcat to be shot, Mother, didn't He? I guess He doesn't like wildcats, does He? But—" the vivid face clouded over—"but, Mother, did God arrange—" the deepening note of anxiety was painfully present— "God didn't arrange for the Bunn boys to drown in the river." The delicate face had gone white, the lips were drawn, the grey hazel eyes staring, the voice fallen to a tremulous, passionate undertone. His little soul was passing into an eclipse of faith. "Whatsoever comes to pass." Against the age-long creed of a God Whose Will runs as the supreme law throughout the universe of men and things, across the wreckage of empires, through seas of blood and tears, working out with serene, unswerving purpose the glory of God, this tender, loving, sensitive heart hurled itself in passionate protest.

"He did not, Mother!" cried the boy, his fists clenched, his eyes ablaze, his voice vibrating in vehement and indignant rage. "He did not arrange them to go. They just went themselves, and their father told them not to. They went themselves. He did not arrange! He did not arrange!" The voice broke in its passionate championing of his God Whom he had seen up next the blue, looking down between the tree tops, with kindly face, the God Whom "he liked awful well" and Who "liked him."

Startled, acutely distressed, the mother sat gazing at the defiantly passionate face: startled to find how intense was her sympathy with that passionate protest of her little lad, distressed that she found no word wherewith to make answer.

"Hello! old chap, what's the row? What's up here?"

A tall man came round the corner of the house, a

photographer's tripod and camera over his shoulder. The boy hesitated a perceptible moment. He stood somewhat in awe of his father, but his passion swept away his fear.

"God did not arrange for the Bunn boys to be drowned in the river, did He, Daddy? They just went themselves, and their father told them not to. God did not arrange it. They did it themselves."

With a swift glance the father took in the salient features of the scene, the pale face of the boy with its trembling lips and burning eyes, the startled, perplexed and distressed face of his mother.

"Certainly, they went themselves," said the father heartily. "They were told not to go, they knew that the high water was dangerous and that the old dugout wasn't safe, but they *would* go. Poor chaps, it was awfully hard lines, but they wouldn't take advice."

"I knew it, I knew it, Daddy!" cried the boy, breaking into a storm of tears. "I knew He wouldn't do anything bad. I just knew He wouldn't hurt anybody——"

The mother caught him in her arms and held him fast.

"Of course He wouldn't, darling. You didn't understand—we none of us understand, but we know He won't do anything unkind, or to hurt us. We are sure of that, we are sure of that." Her own tears were flowing as she rocked the boy in her arms. "But," she added, more to herself than to the boy in her arms, "it is hard to understand"—her eyes wandered up the hillside at the back of the bungalow to a little mound enclosed in a white paling—"no, we can't understand. We will just have to wait, and wait, and be sure He doesn't do anything unkind."

"O' course, I knew He couldn't," said little Paul, snuggling down into her arms.

"I would suggest a more elementary course of theology for a boy of eight—or nine, is he?—dear," said her husband, grinning at her.

"Perhaps we had better stop it," sighed the mother, "at least, for a while. But I did want to go through with it."

"But, my dear, what earthly use is that stuff? I don't say," he hastened to add, reading her face, "it isn't the very finest system of iron-bound, steel-clad theology ever given to mortal mind to chew upon. But, after all, can you reasonably expect the infant there to take in propositions upon which the world's thinkers have been arranged in opposing camps from the great Socrates down to your great little self?"

"And yet, after all, a child is no more puzzled about these mysteries—free will, determinism and all that— than are the best and wisest of men today. So why not give him the formulæ? I think we will go on."

"Well, you know I don't agree. And you know you belong to the ancient pedagogic school in this," chaffed her husband.

"Yes, I know we don't agree," she smiled, "but I would like to go through the Catechism. After all, it is a wonderful little book, you know."

"Wonderful! I should say! Nothing like it has ever been put forth by the human mind. But——"

"Oh, I know all you would say, but I would like to go on——"

"So would I, Mother. And I'm going to go right through, just like you did when you were a little girl. I'm over to 'the sinfulness o' that *mistake* wherein a man fell' and I'll be at 'the misery o' that mistake' next week."

His father shouted.

"Never mind, dear," said the mother, with difficulty controlling her face. "Your father forgets he was a little boy himself once. Indeed, I don't believe he could say the question himself."

"What'll you bet?" said the father. "I learned the thing from cover to cover when I was a kid—got ten bob for saying it before the whole school in a contest."

"Make him say it, Mother," cried the boy, springing

to his feet. "Make him say 'the sinfulness o' that mistake' and 'the misery o' that mistake' too."

Violently protesting, but all in vain, the father was made to repeat not only "the sinfulness of that estate whereinto man fell" but "the misery of that estate" as well, which he did only after some considerable prompting by the delighted boy and his mother.

"So you're going through with it, are you, laddie?" said his father, when he had emerged, somewhat chastened in spirit, from his ordeal.

"Right through to the very end, Daddy, same as Mother did."

"And me too. Don't forget your father's early triumphs. And a lot of good it has done me, eh, Mother?"

"You never know, dear, what good it has done you."

"Or what harm. Luckily I never tried to understand it, like this young philosopher."

"What's a philofisser, Mother?"

"A person who is very fond of knowing things, dear."

"All right, I'm one, Mother. And I'm going to know everything in the Cakism——"

"Catechism, dear."

"Yes, the Catism—all about God and what He does and what He doesn't do too, Mother. 'Specially the things He doesn't do. I don't like those things. Who does arrange the bad things, Mother?"

"Here, youngster, you'll have us all frogging in deep water in another jiffy and shouting for help," said the father. "That'll do. Take your mother up the hill for a walk. It is getting cool enough for a walk, eh, what?"

"I believe I am a little too tired," said the mother, wistfully looking up the hill.

"Oh, go on, Mother. Take it easy. A little walk will do you good."

"Come on, Mother. I'll take care of you," said the boy stoutly.

"Come along then, laddie."

The man stood looking after them as they toiled uphill among the pines, the mother pausing now and again, ostensibly to pick a red lily or to admire some newly opening vista through the aisled forest.

"My God!" he said, through his teeth. "She is getting weaker. She is! She is! We must get her out of this to some one who knows. Must raise the money somehow."

He swore a deep oath, and, passing into the bungalow, sat down to drink his heartache numb in Scotch whiskey.

CHAPTER III

Young Paul Gaspard was eager to be gone for a run up the mountain at the back of the bungalow. Had he known how very nearly the eager light in his grey eyes and the eager emotion quivering in his angel-like face—for so his foolish mother saw it—was to breaking down the resolution that was hardening his mother's voice, he would have turned the full batteries of eyes and face upon her and won.

"No, dear, duty first; pleasure afterwards. Remember Nelson, you know."

"Yes, I know, but Nelson was on a jolly big ship and going into a big fight, Mother. I hate practising—at least," catching the look of surprise and pain which his mother just managed to substitute in time for that of tender pride—"at least, sometimes—and 'specially this morning. It's a perfeckly 'dorable morning."

"The harder the duty, the better the discipline, you know. That's what makes good soldiers, my boy. Come along, get it over. Quick! March! Besides, you know you would just love to get that little *rondo* right—tum te-ta-te-tum di. Let me hear you," said his mother guilefully.

"No, that's wrong, Mother. It's tum-te-ta te tum-di." He ran to the piano and played the phrase.

"Well, what did I say? Oh, yes, I see, the phrasing was wrong. How does it go?"

In a minute the boy was absorbed in his *rondo*. His mother sat in the sunlit window listening to the practising. Her face was worn and lined with pain. But as she listened, watching the long clever fingers flitting so surely and smoothly over the keys, the lines of pain and weari-

21

ness seemed to be filled in with warm waves of light. She lay back in her easy chair, knowing herself to be unobserved, and gave herself over to a luxurious hour of loving pride in her son. He had a true feeling for what was fine and sound in music and a gift of interpretation extraordinary for one of his age. It was his heritage from his father who in his youth had discovered to his instructors a musical ability amounting almost to genius. Had he possessed that element in genius which is a capacity for taking pains he undoubtedly would have made a great artist on the piano.

"If your father had been made to practise he would have been a great player," his mother would say to Paul, on occasions when, thrilled to the heart, they sat drinking the weird and mystic beauty of the "Moonlight" flowing from his fingers.

"Yes, boy," the father would reply, "if I only had had a stern and relentless taskmistress for a mother, such as you have, eh?" And then the boy and his mother would look at each other and smile.

Now the mother was listening and watching while her son did one of Mozart's Sonatinas with fine touch and expression.

"You do that quite well, dear," she said when the Sonatina was over. "That will do now. You will run to the top of the hill, to the big pine root and then we shall do our lessons——"

"Let me do this Minuet first, Mother. I just feel like it now."

"No, dear, you've had enough—indeed more than enough. A little fresh air, and then your lessons for an hour, then out."

"Just this Minuet, Mother, dear."

"Duty first, boy, you know."

"Why, Mother, that's what you said when you sent me to the piano; now it's the same thing when you want me to quit!"

"Yes, dear, duty first always—the thing to be done at

the time it ought to be done and in the way it ought to be done."

"My, it's awful hard, Mother. Can't I ever do just as I like?"

"Why, yes, dear."

"When? When I grow big like you?"

"Oh, before that, I hope. When you want to do the things you ought to do. But now, out you go for your run, up to the pine root and back again. I'll time you." She pulled out her watch. The little lad, every muscle taut, set himself.

"All set!" she cried. "Ready! Go!"

As if released from a spring the lithe little body shot forward and disappeared through the underbrush. She waited for him, watch in hand, waited, thinking, then forgot him. The minutes went on unheeded, so too her mind. Down the years it went, following that lithe figure, that eager shining face gallantly fronting the unknown, unafraid and alone. She could not see herself with him. She knew, she had faced the knowledge steadily till she could face it calmly, she knew her vision of that gallant and lonely figure would soon, too soon, be realised. His father—somehow she could not see them together. They were not made for the same path. Hugh, her dear, splendid, happy hearted, easy-going man, was made for the smooth ways through the low lands, but her boy she always saw with face lifted up to the heights. He would never be content with the levels. The hills, yes, and the mountains were for him. And hence he must go alone. As for her, she was tired, unfit, nearly done. No heights for her, but rest, deep, still and comforting. Well, she knew she would find it; of that she had no fear. And the deep heart-break of leaving all this light and warmth and love, that had made life to her, she had surmounted. She had allowed her eyes to follow her son's and through the clouds next the blue she had seen a face that seemed kind and she had grown content. An infinite comfort had stolen over her aching heart that Sunday not so long ago as she thought over her little boy's quaint words, "And I like Him, Mother, and I think He likes me." Alone she might be, and alone her little boy might be, but never quite alone after all would either be, no matter where the path might lead. With a start she came back to the present hour. She looked at her watch. The boy had been gone thirty minutes, instead of ten at the most. She was not alarmed. The woods were safe, and she knew her boy. Young as he was, she knew he was without fear and could be depended upon to do the wise thing. But where was he? She set off slowly toward the big pine root. The April sun was kindly in its warmth, the pine needles dry under foot, and the air was rich with the aroma of the pines. She moved quietly through the brush, saving her strength, as she had need, with her ear alert for a sound of her little lad. In a few minutes she heard his joyous shout. He had caught sight of her through an opening in the bush, and came tearing through toward her.

"Mother! Mother," he shouted, "the baby is choking, Mother! dying! Come! oh, come quick! Mother."

"What are you talking about, Paul? Don't shout, speak quietly." She held him firmly, speaking calmly. "What baby, and where is it?"

"Oh, Mother, it's——"

"Stop, Paul! Now, quietly——"

The boy took hold of himself and began in a quiet voice. "Yes, Mother. The baby is up in the woods by the big root. It is an Indian baby, and it is choking."

"Show me the way."

With all the speed she could make she followed the boy, and in a few minutes came upon a pathetic little group, a young Indian woman, exquisitely beautiful in face and form, a mere girl she seemed, kneeling before a child of four, lying on a blanket, with face deeply cyanosed and distorted, looking like death.

"What is the matter?" she cried, kneeling beside the girl. "Has the child swallowed anything?"

"No, no," said the mother, speaking perfect English in the soft, low musical Indian voice. "It is croup, I think. He has had a bad cold, he has been bad all night. He will die." Her words came with the passionless calm of despair.

"No, he must not die," said Mrs. Gaspard. "Paul, now listen carefully. I depend on you."

"Yes, Mother," said her son, standing looking at her, quiet, alert, tense.

"Run to Jinny, tell her to fill the bath half full with hot water."

Like a bird in flight he was off through the woods.

"Come! Bring your baby!" she said to the Indian girl.

Swiftly, without a word, the mother caught up the child and followed Mrs. Gaspard to the house. For an hour they fought with death, and won. Exhausted by the struggle, Mrs. Gaspard retired to her own room to rest. Paul she sent off on his pony for a scamper. Beside her child, now quietly sleeping, the Indian woman sat, staring out of the window, motionless, passionless, as if she were a carved image, heedless to all about her.

Thus the morning hours passed, till at the approach of noon the voices of Paul and his father were heard from the paddock near the house. At the first sound of the man's voice the Indian girl leaped to the window, flung one swift glance at the man's face, stood one moment, trembling, uncertain, then with quick resolve gathered up her sleeping boy in his blanket and with the fleet and silent movements of the wild things of the forest she slipped from the room out of the house and disappeared into the brushwood at the rear.

Full of excited chatter, Paul conducted his father into the house, and, subduing his voice, led him into the kitchen where he had left the Indian woman and her child.

"Where is she?" he exclaimed. He ran out into the

summer kitchen where Jinny was at work over the wash tub. "Where are they gone—the Indian woman?"

"Are they no there?" said Jinny, coming into the kitchen, wiping her dripping arms. "They'll be ben the hoose. Hush, now, y're mither is resting," she added, passing into the living room, followed by Paul.

"They're gone," said Paul aghast, "and with that sick baby."

"Aye," said Jinny grimly, "and I hope there was no need for hurry."

"What do you mean, Jinny?" asked Mr. Gaspard. "Oh, I see. Well, you need not fear. Indians do not steal."

"Steal?" said Paul, his face aflame with indignation. "I think it is just mean to appose she would steal. She is a good woman, and she just kissed and kissed Mother's hands for curing her baby."

"Aw, weel, I'd lippen till nane o' them."

"Steady, Paul," interposed his father. "Jinny doesn't know them as we do. We will investigate a bit. Where did you find her?"

"I'll show you, Daddy," said Paul, hurling a blighting look upon Jinny, who returned undisturbed to her tub.

Together they hurried up the path toward the big pine root. Arrived there, the cry of a child lured them farther up the hill. Paul was off like a hound on the trail. In a very few moments his voice came back through the bushes in remonstrance.

"Why are you going away? Your baby will be sick again. Mother wants you to stay. Daddy's here. Wait! Wait! Here, Daddy! Here she is!"

Dashing back through the bushes, he seized his father and dragged him hurriedly to where the Indian woman stood. She had flung her bundle of camp impedimenta to the ground and, with her child rolled up in the blanket, she stood like a wild animal fiercely at bay.

"Onawata!" gasped the man, and stood gazing at her, speechless, for some seconds. Then with a quick glance at the boy he spoke rapidly in Indian. Fiercely she replied. Again the man spoke, pointing to the child. For reply she flung toward him an accusing finger. As if she had struck him in the face, the man stood, white, aghast, rooted in his tracks.

"Paul," he said in a voice harsh and shaken, "go back to the house and tell Mother——"

"Is the baby dead?" said the boy in an awed voice.

"Dead? Dead?" said his father. "Would to God—— No! Nonsense! Dead? No fear!" he added with a harsh laugh.

"Let me see," said the boy, springing forward and pulling the blanket from the face of the child. "No, he's all right. See, Daddy! Isn't he lovely?"

The man glanced at the child, shuddered, then with an obvious effort pulled himself together.

"He's quite all right, Paul. Run back now and tell Mother I am—I have gone to see them safe to their camp." He spoke a few words to the woman. "Yes, about a mile down the valley. All right, old chap! I'll be right back," he added kindly. "Off you go now. Cut away!"

"Come," he said to the woman, picking up her bundle, as Paul reluctantly turned away homeward. For some minutes Gaspard strode in silence along the trail, followed by the woman, then flinging down the bundle he faced her.

"Why have you come here?" he said sternly in Indian.

"Why did you not tell me you had a woman, a wife?" replied the woman, her voice low, soft, but firm as his own.

"You speak good English," he answered, astonished. "Where did you learn?"

"I spent two years at the mission school. I worked hard, very hard. I wanted to——" She hesitated, and then added in a bitter tone. "I made a mistake. I thought you were a good man. I did not know you."

For a few minutes the man stood voiceless before her. He was not a bad man, much less a heartless man. Five years ago, on a hunting trip in the far north land, as the result of an accident he had made a long stay with a band of Chippewayan Indians, the lords of the Athabasca country. Cared for and nursed back to strength in the wigwam of the chief, he had played the villain as many another white man had, without thought of consequence. Today he stood convicted, appalled in the presence, not of a squaw who could be easily appeased with gifts and who would think herself very well off were the gifts sufficiently generous, but of a woman, beautiful, proud, speaking his own tongue with ease and, in her soft Indian intonation, even with charm. In her arms was his child, a fact stubborn, insistent of recognition, with possibility of overwhelming disaster.

For in his mind the one thought obliterating all others was that of his wife. Should this terrible and shameful fact come to her knowledge, what would be the result? He pictured the reaction in her, of horror, loathing, repulsion. For well he knew her lofty sense of right, her Puritan holiness of spirit. She would despise him beyond hope of restoring. She could never bear to look upon him, much less allow him to touch her. She would pity him, but never more could she regard him with that adoring love which had been to him the supreme joy and satisfaction of his life. Without her love, life for him would be over. His mind, with one swift, comprehending glance, scanned the future years, and from the desolation his soul shrank back in fear. No! If she came to know, there was only one way out for him—the coward's way, but he would take it. He could meet hell, but life without her love and with her pity and loathing would be worse than any hell he could imagine.

There was one thing to do and that quickly. He must get this woman away out of this country, back to her own. Once buried there, he could draw the breath of freedom again. Of her fate and the fate of the child he took no heed. In his horror and terror of the impending calamity of discovery he could have killed them both where they stood and buried them in that remote valley. Swiftly his mind played with that possibility. It could be done. His eye fell upon the handle of the hatchet sticking out of her bundle. One blow, two, and all cause of fear would be forever gone from his life. He took a step toward the hatchet. Aghast, he came to himself. "My God, what has come to me?" he cried aloud, stepping back as if from the very mouth of the bottomless pit. "Not that! The other perhaps, but not that!" He cast his eyes about him. This was still his world, with all its familiar sights. The sun was shining, far down there swept the valley of the Windermere, the hills, the pines. In what strange, God-cursed country had his soul been wandering? To him it seemed that years had passed. He had been companying with devils. What had come upon him? What sort of man had he become? And what might he not yet be driven to? He had read of such transformations in good, well-meaning, decent, kindly men. Would he become so demonised? Demonised! Now he understood, now he instantly believed in the possibility of demon possession. The man with the legion of devils was no myth, but a terrible reality. Trembling throughout his powerful frame, he stood fighting for self-recovery.

A wailing cry struck upon his senses like the crash of a thunder peal. He sprang forward, caught the child from the mother's arms, rolled it in its blanket, seized the bundle, and with the single word "Come!" set off through the woods at a terrific pace, the Indian woman following. For an hour without a word from either he smashed his way through the underbrush, down valleys, over rocky ledges, one thought only driving him as the furies Orestes—to get away from his wife. He had a vague, blind notion that he would make the Athabasca before he halted. He would have gone on thus, blindly, madly, had not a cry again arrested him. The child in his

arms began to squirm, struggle, fight for liberty, scream-
ing lustily the while. The mother caught his arm.

"Give me my boy," she said breathlessly.

Whirling upon her he gave the child into her arms,
flung down the bundle and stood facing her.

"Where is your camp?" he asked abruptly.

"Down on the river, at the big rapid," she said quietly,
busying herself with the child.

"Who are there?"

"My father and two of his men."

He continued gazing at her as if she were a stranger to
him. He was wet to the skin. His hair was plastered
in curls about his forehead.

"You must go home," he said, his voice grating harshly.
"Why did you come here?"

She continued her task of caring for the child. She
too was trembling, but not with her mad chase after
him. The hour's strenuous exertion had hardly quickened her breathing. All day marches, carrying her bundle
and her child, were to her nothing unusual. It was the
passion in her that shook her like a palsy.

"Why did you come?" repeated the man. "What do
you want?"

She set down the child. Her trembling hands suddenly
grew steady. Her face settled into stern lines of calm.
Her voice came in the quiet strength of a deep flowing
river. She was past all fear, past desire, past hope. She
was in full command of herself, of the situation, of him
too.

"Two months ago I left my country because I had
here," she laid her hand on her breast, "a great pain to
see your face again, to hear you speak, to touch your
hand. That is gone, all gone, gone like the snow of last
year from the mountains. Today my heart is dead. I
have seen your woman. I have seen your face. You
have no thought, no love for the Indian girl. To you
she is like the dead leaves—nothing! nothing! You would
kill her and her child. I saw death in your eyes just now.

I go away, back to the Athabasca. You will never see my face again. But before I go I ask you one thing. This boy, this little boy"—for an instant the even calm of her voice was shaken—"he is my son, but first he is your son. What will he be, Indian or white man? The Indian is like the buffalo and the deer. The white man is hunting him from the plains and the woods. Soon he will be like the mountain sheep, only in the lonely valleys or the far mountain tops. What will your boy be? Where will he go? I wait for your voice."

The man stood listening, held as by a spell. The anger passed from his face. In its place came in swift succession relief, surprise, perplexity, shame, humiliation. Before her superb self-abnegation he stood self-condemned, mean, contemptible. He could find no words. This girl who had in those careless days so long ago worshipped him as a god and given herself to him with never a care or question had changed into a woman, his equal in truth of feeling, in sense of right. Here she was asking his solution of a problem that was his before it was hers, and his more than hers. The boy? The little chap standing up straight on sturdy legs, gazing at him with piercing, solemn, appraising eyes—his boy? His heart gave a queer little quiver. Indian or white man? Condemned to be hunted back beyond the horizon of civilisation? Or trained, fitted for a chance for life among men? Never in his life had his thoughts raced through his mind as today in the presence of this girl, this grave, controlled woman by whose very calmness he stood accused and condemned as by a judge upon the bench. For his very life, with those clear, calm eyes reading his soul, he could make no answer. There was no answer in his mind. His first thought had been that the Indian woman should simply disappear from his world and find a home with her own people. But as he listened to her quiet and reasoned appeal in her quaintly picturesque speech, the product of the mission school, and as he looked upon her face, alight with clear-seeing intelligence, aglow with the divine light of motherhood and distinguished with a beauty beyond any he had ever known, the solution which first suggested itself to his mind somehow failed to satisfy. Then, too, the boy, the little boy—his little son—for whom he was responsible before God—yes, and, if it were known to them, before all honourable men, and that meant in his own sight. Was man ever so cornered by fate, nay, by his own doings?

"I will see you tomorrow, Onawata," he said more gently. "I will come to your camp tomorrow." He laid his hand upon her shoulder. At his touch and at the change in his voice, the woman was transformed, as if in a single moment the world should pass from the cold beauty of winter to the warm living glory of a midsummer day. Under the brown skin the red blood surged, rich and full, lending warmth and color to the cold beauty of her face. The rigid lines in her slim straight body suddenly seemed to melt into soft curves of winsome grace. The dark steadfast eyes grew soft as with a yearning tenderness. With a little shuddering sigh she sank upon the pine needles, her hands fluttering up toward him.

"Ah, ah, Wa-ka-no-ka" (Hunter with the Golden Hair), she said, with a long sobbing cry. "Do not speak so to me, do not touch me, or I cannot go back. Ah, how can I leave you unless you hate me?"

She swayed forward toward him, flung her arms about his ankles and held him fast, sobs deep drawn shaking her body.

Gaspard was not a hard man. Rather was he strongly, keenly susceptible of appeal to the æsthetic and emotional elements in his artistic nature. The sight of this woman, young—she was not more than twenty-two—beautiful and pitifully, hopelessly, his slave as well as his victim, moved him deeply. He leaned down over her, lifted her to her feet and, with his arms thrown about her, sought to stay her sobbing.

"Don't, child," he said. "Don't cry like that. We

will find some way out of the mess, or, by God," he added with sudden passion, "we'll make one."

Still sobbing, she leaned against him. The absence of any suggestion of passion in him revealed to her woman's instinct that the dream that had drawn her from her far north home was madness. She knew she was nothing to him and could be nothing to him. Her very despair quieted her, and she stood, limp and drooping, her eyes on the ground, her hands folded before her.

"Come, I will take you to your camp, and tomorrow I will talk with you," said Gaspard, with a gentle kindness in his voice and manner.

The girl roused herself, glanced about to discover her child who was busying himself among the bushes, then turning back to him said with a simple and quiet dignity, "No, you must not come. I do not need you. I must do without you. It is all past. Now you go back to your woman. Tomorrow you will tell me about your boy." She rolled the child up in his blanket, slung him Indian fashion over her shoulder, picked up her bundle and with never another look at the man and with never a word she took her way.

"Tomorrow," said Gaspard, "I shall see you. Goodbye."

Unheeding, she passed on down the trail, and the underbrush hid her from his sight.

CHAPTER IV

The burden upon the man's soul grew heavier with every step homeward. He was going to meet his wife, the woman he had wronged, the woman who was to him the very centre of his being, the dearest of all he possessed in life, without whose respect and love life would lose its meaning and value. As to the Indian woman and her wrong, truth to tell, though he pitied her, he felt no very acute concern. True enough, the astonishing advance she had made during the past five years in the white man's civilisation and culture had given her a new place in his consideration. She was no longer an ignorant squaw whose rights and wrongs could be estimated in terms purely materialistic. She had developed a mind and a soul. The memory of that appeal of hers for her son, for his son, calm, dignified, pungent, still shook him. But his chief concern now was how to bury this whole wretched business from the knowledge of his wife beyond possibility of resurrection.

The picture of his wife's face following the possible revelation of his sin halted him in his stride and wrung from his soul's depths a groan.

"My God! My God!" he cried aloud, lifting his hands heavenward. "Let that never come! Let that never come!"

Sooner death to her, to him, and, as for the Indian and her child, to them death a thousand times. He wiped the sweat from his face and stood gazing about him. How changed the whole world was within a brief two hours' space! The same mountains, trees, river, sun and sky, yet to him all seemed flooded with a new light, lurid and awesome. Yet it was not his sin, but the dread terror of detection, of its consequences, that had wrought this change in his world. He could not keep his wife's face out of his mind. Her dark blue reproachful eyes, sad and horror-stricken, were holding him in relentless grip. He dreaded facing her. His artistic and highly emotional temperament, his power of vivid imagination, gave living reality to the picture. He flung his hands again high above his head.

"God in Heaven, this is madness!" he exclaimed. "Madness, sheer, fool madness! She will never know. How can she know?"

He shivered and stamped, as if smitten with midwinter cold. He glanced about him. A warm and sunny ledge of rock carpeted with moss and pine needles invited him. He threw himself down upon it, pulled out his pipe, deliberately filled it from his pouch and struck a match. The flame shook in his fingers. He cursed himself for a fool. He was acting like a frightened child. He raged at himself and his weak folly. He must take a grip of himself. His pipe helped him to a more normal mood. The mere performance of the familiar physical act of sucking in and exhaling the smoke helped him. He held up his hand before him. The discovery that his hand was no longer shaking helped him. He stretched himself at full length upon the sunny ledge and let his eyes wander over the scene spread out before him. Unconsciously, the wild, wide, lonely beauty of the landscape reached his soul and quieted him. His artist's eye began to select, group, compose into a picture, the elements in this wonder world before him. The very tensity of his nervous condition aided him. His mind was working with swift constructive power.

"Lord! What a light! What colour!" he said, as his eye rested upon the rich deep purple in the hollows of the hills on the far side of the valley. He longed for his brushes. His fingers dived into the pocket of his jacket for his sketch book, without which he never walked abroad. In another moment he was deep in his work, sketching with swift, sure fingers, filling in the outlines, noting the colours, the lights, the shadows, the fall of foothills from the great mountain peaks, the serried lines of the pines at the horizon, the broad silver ribbon of the river, the tawny gold of the grassy levels. He had an hour of absorbing delight in his work.

"There! Never did anything finer!" he exulted. He rapidly reviewed his work, re-touching, emphasising, correcting.

"I'll get that into colour at once," he muttered, thrusting his book into his pocket. The act recalled him to the grim reality of his situation.

He was surprised to discover that most of its horror had somehow gone. He was immensely relieved.

"What a baby I am!" he said, with a smile of complacent self-pity. "What an emotional, imaginative ass!" But even as he spoke he felt the shadows creeping again over the landscape of his soul.

"Here! Enough of this!" he exclaimed, springing to his feet. "I'm going to face this thing like a man. I played the fool. I'll do the right thing by the girl—and her baby."

Her baby? His mind was away on a new tack, like a ship caught by a sudden shift of wind. His baby? His son? Indian or white? Or half-breed? What! His son! Truly, he was in a devilish cleft. Well he knew, none better, for he had lived with and worked with him, that, of all the human beings roving the new country, the half-breed, in spite of many splendid exceptions which he had met, was the most to be pitied, the most despicable. Too often inheriting the weaknesses and vices of both races, he was the derelict of the borderland of civilisation. Settled down upon the land, as in the Red River Valley, he could climb to strength and honour among the white race. Roving the plains and the woods with the tribes, he frequently sank beneath their level, more easily accessible to the vices of the white man, unable and unwilling to attain to the splendid and unspoiled

nobility of the red man in his native wilds. Indian or
white man? Again he could hear that calm, passionless
voice putting to him the alternative, clearly he visualised
those steady, relentless eyes holding his with unwavering
grip. The problem was his, not hers. Alone, she would,
she must find the only solution possible; his son would
be Indian—no, not even Indian, but half-breed. He was
conscious of a fearful shrinking from that alternative.
He had a very clear picture of the little chap, with his
straight back, his sturdy legs, his shy, dark, yet fearless
eyes, the curl to his hair. No! He would give the boy
a chance! With a mother like that he had a right to a
chance. He would have him educated. Trader—trapper
—rancher—there were many possibilities open to him of
escape from the degradation of the roving half-breed,
haunting the Indian wigwam, slinking round the saloons
of the frontier village. He would give him a chance.
He would keep a distant eye upon him. The little chap
should have his full opportunity, for manhood, for Canadian citizenship. After all, it would be easy enough.
The whole thing could be arranged to do justice to every
one involved.

He smiled at his recent terror. But again, even as he
smiled, deep within him there was an uneasy stirring that
his terrors would come upon him again when his mood
had changed. For the present he had shaken from him
his fear. He would meet his wife with a quiet face and
a steady eye. He sprang to his feet. He must get home
quickly. The lunch hour was long since past, and ex-
planations would be expected. Well, they were easy: he
had carried the woman's bundle to her camp by the Big
Rapid. He set off, whistling bravely a merry lilt. A
sudden memory killed the song at his lips. There was
his son Paul. He had witnessed the meeting with the
Indian woman. Just what had been said and done, he
could not well remember, the shock of the meeting had
been so overpowering. The boy's powers of perception
were uncanny and, too, he was free of speech, terribly

so.   What had he noticed?   What were the boy's thoughts about that meeting and conversation?   That there had been previous acquaintance had been made clear.   Had he not called her by her Indian name?   He was almost sure he had.   He could not deny acquaintance.   Well! It was safest not to deny too much.   Of course, he had met her and her people in his wanderings, had hunted with her tribe—very decent lot they were too, they had done him a good turn and were great friends of his. There must be no mystery about this.   Yes, he would take Paul to visit their camp some day, as doubtless the boy would demand.   But he would take care that the camp would be deserted on the day of the visit.   It was all simple enough.   Why make such a fuss about it?   The main consideration was to get the Indian woman and her people out of the country with all speed, and that he could accomplish without much difficulty.   When he had arrived at this satisfactory conclusion, however, he made the disturbing discovery that that vast sense of relief, that scorn of himself and of his childish terror, which had cheered him half an hour ago, had largely evaporated from his spirit, and once more the haunting dread of discovery was upon him.   Once more he found himself visualising the accusing face, the steady, disquieting eye of his wife.   Again he cursed himself for a fool.

"Imagination!   My damned imagination!" he muttered, as he smashed his way through the bushes.   "Look here, this will not do," he said aloud, coming to a dead stop.   "I must get hold of myself."

Resolutely he slowed his pace.   Suddenly with a sickening sinking of heart, it came upon him that henceforth throughout his life he must carry this haunting load of fear.   He would never be without it.   Be it so!   He would carry it as a man should.   He would face the fear and fight it.   He would play the man for his own sake, but more for the sake of the woman to whom he was now going with his lie and who stood to him for all that was best in life.   For his boy's sake too.   No shadow would he suffer to fall on them if he had to go through hell itself for it. This resolve steadied him, and with this resolve he arrived at his own back door. His son's shout welcomed him.

"Hello, Daddy! Where are they? Where is their camp? Will you take me to see them?"

"Who? Oh, the Indians! Yes, they are safely at their camp. Long way off though. I'll take you some day. I say, I am hungry! Lunch over?"

"Yes, Daddy, we couldn't wait any longer. Where is the camp? Do you know them? Where did you meet them? Mother," he shouted, as she came to the door, "Daddy's going to take me to the Indian camp."

"Why did she run away like that, Hugh? That little boy needs care. He will be having another attack. They should be under shelter."

He glanced at her face. How worn and ill and worried she looked!

"Oh, don't you worry about that little chap. You can't kill those Indians. They're all right. Very decent lot they are," he went on nonchalantly, "better than most. Father's quite a superior old boy. Chippewayans they are. Met them some time ago. Did some hunting with them. But here! I'm hungry as a hawk, starving, ravenous, dangerous. Anything left to eat? Oh, by the way, got a fine picture this morning on my way back. Wonderful thing—lights just right. Must get it down this afternoon before I forget."

"Come, Hugh, never mind your picture now. You must be famished. Come along. I've kept your lunch hot for you. It is quite spoiled, of course, but——" Her arms went about his neck. He could hardly repress a shudder as he received her kisses.

"Never mind, Mother," he said brusquely, "it will be the best ever. Let me splash my face a bit. Run off, Paul, now. After lunch we will have a walk."

"Oh, splendid! To the camp, to see the Indians?" shouted the boy. "I adore Indians. What——"

"Off you go, boy, and let me get through with my lunch. Vamoose! Clear out! Do you hear?" he shouted at the boy with mock fierceness.

Thank God, the first meeting was safely over. He had carried it off successfully. His spirits rose with a bound. He must get them thinking of something else. Preoccupation was the idea. His new picture! He would put some hard hours upon that. His wife would be interested and pleased. She always was when he really worked at his easel, and more especially when he carried the thing through to completion. He would put the finishing touches to this picture. The scene began to come back to him. He brought his sketch book to the lunch table with him.

"There is the making of a great picture, Marion," he cried, opening out the book for her.

Eagerly she came to his side, and stood with her hand on his shoulder.

"Show me, dear," she said. Her tenderness was like a knife in him.

"See that line of mountains in the far distance, wonderful blue at the sky line, and down the sides in the hollows and at the base purple. My dear! Such purple —shot through with rose tints!" He grew enthusiastic.

"There, that will do, Hugh!" she said, taking away his sketch book from him and patting his head as if he were a little boy. "Lunch just now, and then you will get at your picture right after. You are starved. Your lunch is spoiled, I fear, but it is the very best Jinny could do."

All through lunch he talked eagerly, excitedly, about his picture. His art work always excited him, and when a scene really gripped his imagination he was mad to be at it. He hurried through his meal, seized his sketch book, and in a minute was busy with his palette. An hour later his wife came in to him and, sitting down in an easy chair, watched him at his work. Back and forward, with quick step and with eager, clever fingers, he touched and re-touched, spreading upon the canvas the scene of the morning, with never a pause and never an erasure. He had rarely worked so surely, rarely with such mastery in his brush.

"Splendid! Hugh, wonderful!" said his wife. Something in her voice arrested his swiftly moving brush. He faced about and glanced at her. Her face was ashen. His heart sank with a terrible fear—did she suspect anything?

"Marion, you are ill," he cried, flinging down his brush and palette. "What is it?"

"Nothing much, dear," she said wearily. "I am tired a bit. The morning has been a little trying."

"What do you mean, darling?"

"The Indian woman," she said faintly.

"The Indian woman?" he echoed, his voice as faint as her own. Had the thing he dreaded come to pass? "What do you mean?"

Then she told him of her experience with the sick child and the fight with death, in which she had played the chief rôle.

"It was a very serious case, Hugh," she said. "It made me think of our little Marie. The little fellow was just gone when I got him into the tub. He must be a very, very strong child, stronger than——"

He was immensely relieved for the moment.

"But, my dear Marion, you have knocked yourself up. You are all in, I say. And all for a little Indian brat——"

"Oh, Hugh! He was a perfect darling. I never saw a more lovely, a more perfect little body—and so fair for an Indian."

"But it nearly killed you." His recent scare and his anxiety for his wife's condition made him savage. "You should not have done it. You know well you cannot stand excitement."

"Dear Hugh," she said, drawing his head down to her breast, "I love you when you are in a rage like this. But, darling boy," she paused a few moments. "I am going to tell you something, and promise me you will be very, very brave. Indeed, you must be brave, for I am such a coward. I fear there is something wrong, terribly wrong with me. I have had such a strange, heavy pain here for so long." She laid her hand upon her stomach. "I am afraid, Hugh, afraid." Her voice died away in a whisper.

He was about to break forth into indignant, scornful protest against such nonsense, but when he looked into her face his words died at his lips, his heart grew cold and he could only continue gazing at her.

"Don't, Hugh!" she cried. "You must not look like that, or I cannot bear it."

For answer he groaned like a man who has been stricken with a death wound, put his arms round her and held her in a shuddering embrace. For a moment or two his world had gone black, but only for a moment or two.

"No, Marion," he said, with resolute voice, "we shall not yield to our fears. You gave me an awful shock. There may be something quite seriously wrong. It would be foolish to say anything else. I have seen you failing in strength for a few months past. But we are not going to give up. There are wonderful doctors in the world today. We are going to fight and fight with all we've got to fight with."

"Thank you, dear Hugh. You are a brave man." Then she added brightly, "I want you to do something for me today."

"Anything! Today or any day," he said fervently. "I only hope it is hard enough. What is it, dear?"

"Finish that picture. You know your failing, dear. It is going to be wonderful."

He looked at her aghast. "You have surely asked a hard one," he murmured.

"I know, dear, but I want to sit here and watch that picture grow under your hands till it is quite perfect. Come, Hugh, I am feeling better. I have been feeling much better the last few weeks. It was the sudden excitement and the heavy work this morning. The little chap is quite a weight, you know. I shall be better to-morrow. Now, get to work, dear boy. See, that light over the left background is too high, I think."

Dully his eyes followed her finger, as she pointed out defects and excellencies in the picture. Suddenly he picked up his brush.

"I'll do it! I'll finish it for your sake! I haven't often done it, but I'll finish this before I do a stroke of anything else."

There was still abundance of light throughout the long spring afternoon, while hour after hour he wrought at his canvas under the inspiration of a great scene, listening to his wife's approving or critical comments, discussing with her lights and shadows, distance, composition, balance, giving her the while a simple and perfect joy. As the best of the light failed she drew him away from his easel and, after tea, out into the soft spring evening.

There was something very tender in their love for each other that evening. It was an hour that Gaspard never forgot for all the following years of his life. In his wife there was an almost unreal buoyancy of spirit in reaction from her depression of the morning, a subtle sweetness of charm, a delicate tenderness that brought back to him the early days of their betrothal when just to hear her speak, to watch the color come into her cheek, to catch the mystic, meaningful look in her eye, which he knew was for him alone, had been wont to work in him a joy beyond words to express, an exaltation of imaginative ecstasy which had power to turn Glasgow's muddy streets and solidly dull tenements into "pathways of silver and palaces of gold." Slowly they walked down the driveway, under the tall red pines which now were standing like rigid sentinels in the windless silence of the soft spring air. Far across the valley stood the distant mountains, now showing dark blue in clean-cut outline against a sky of wonderful, quivering liquid gold, and between the mountains and the bench of foothills on which stood their home lay the broad valley still deep in soft yellow sunshine reflected from the sky overhead, except where the shadows from the mountain peaks fell in long dark lances and where the masses of the pine tops showed a deep blue black. A hushed stillness had fallen upon the world, except for the exquisite notes of the meadow lark which now and then fell upon the silent air, liquid and golden, as from no other living bird in any known land. As they walked thus beneath the pines, holding each other's hand like children, the sweet sad beauty of the dying day, the mystic silence of the wide valley at their feet, the deep shadow of the pines splashed with wide pools of gold, the liquid bell-like note of the bird, like a voice from another world, all together brought a great ease to strained nerves and tortured hearts.

"It is a good world, Hugh, a dear, good world," said his wife as they stood together drinking in with all their senses the beauty, the glory, the soft tender silence of the falling evening.

"The best ever," replied her husband, "if only——"

"Oh, let's have no 'if' today. I've had a wonderful afternoon. You've given me a wonderful afternoon, Hugh. I won't forget it ever."

"Forget what?"

"How good you are to me, Hugh," she said.

"Good to you? Good Lord! But I mean to be! I want to be! You can bank on that." His voice grew uncertain.

"I do, I do. I know it well," she said.

"And you will always believe that?" he asked with a strange intensity. "Always? No matter what comes?" He threw his arm about her.

"Hugh, I believe you are making love to me." She laughed happily.

"God knows I am," he said with emphasis. "And God knows that never will I do anything else than make love to you, so long as I live. I am really only beginning to love you."

"What? You dare to tell me that you have been deceiving me all these dozen years?"

"Of course I imagined I loved you. But I was only a boy and I was only beginning to know you. Indeed, I am only beginning to know you now."

Again she laughed, a happy laugh, the laugh of a care-free light-hearted girl.

"How serious you are, Hugh, old boy! Let us be happy."

They returned to the verandah and there, while the night came up from behind the distant hills, they sat watching in almost complete silence, needing no words for perfect fellowship, till old Jinny brought in a dirty and very weary boy to say good-night.

CHAPTER V

Hugh Gaspard rose next morning with his mind set upon the accomplishment of his tasks. First he must finish his picture, and then he must get that Indian woman away from the country. Both of these things must be done and done today. Before all else he must finish the picture, because it had gripped him and he could not escape from it, but chiefly because he was somehow conscious of an overmastering eagerness to do what he knew would bring to his wife's face that look of joy and pride in him which during the last twenty-four hours had become intensely desirable. It was as if he had a foreboding that for him that look might never appear again.

The morning hours his wife spent in bed, hearing Paul's lessons. Through the open doors of her bedroom and his studio he could hear their voices, the high, clear, eager, questioning voice of the boy and the gentle tones of the mother in reply. Coming into the living room for a fresh supply of tobacco, he heard the boy reciting the Catechism which was always the first lesson in the morning.

"Every sin *a*serveth God's wrath and curse, both in this life and that which is *a*come——"

"*To* come, dear," corrected the mother.

"To come," repeated Paul. "Does that mean in hell, Mother?" the clear, high voice demanded cheerfully.

There was a pause, then, "Yes, dear. Now say it again, 'What does every sin deserve?'" The answer was given with fair correctness.

"But God doesn't ever send any one to hell, Mother, does He? Asa Sleeman says it's a fire worse'n the lime kiln—an' He wouldn't do that, would He? He couldn't, you know."

"What makes you think so, dear?" asked the mother anxiously. The man listened, breathless.

"Because no one would ever sin more'n four hundred and ninety times a day, would he? An' that means in half a day, because he sleeps almost half a day, and that would be four hundred and ninety times in half a day."

"What in the world do you mean, Paul? Four hundred and ninety times?"

"Why, Mother, don't you remember what Jesus said to the asciples?" Paul had difficulty with his dental and other initial consonants.

"What was that? I forget," replied the bewildered mother.

"Oh, Mother, I didn't appose you would forget that— our very last lesson."

"Read it to me, Paul," said the gentle voice.

"Here it is, Mother," cried the boy. The father could hear him turning the leaves of the big Bible. "'Then came Peter and said to Him, Lord, how oft shall my brother sin against me, and I forgive him? Until seven times? Jesus said unto him, I say not unto thee, Until seven times; but, Until seventy times seven.' There, Mother—'Seventy times seven,' four hundred and ninety times," cried the boy triumphantly. "And everybody is sorry some time for his sins, isn't he? Anyway, He said four hundred and ninety times, so that's all right. Four hundred and ninety times in one day; that's from seven to seven, acause he couldn't sin in his sleep, Mother. So I guess He'd just forgive the very worstest man in the whole world, wouldn't He, Mother?"

"Yes, dear, I believe he would." There was a note of joyous relief in her voice. She had escaped once more from another of those terrible theological dilemmas into which her eager young son was so frequently forcing her.

"I know He would acause you would me. Mother, would you, four hundred and ninety times in one day?"

"Yes, dear."

"Five hundred times?"

"Yes, dear."

"A thousand million times?"

"Yes, dear, you know I would."

"An' God's just as good as you, Mother, isn't He?"

"Oh, my dear, don't say that. I am not good."

"You are, Mother," shouted the boy indignantly. "You're just as good as God."

"Hush, dear, hush! Don't speak like that. God is perfect, you know. No! No! Don't say that again."

"All right, Mother, but I know all the same. Anyway, seventy times seven is four hundred and ninety."

"Yes, my boy, always remember that as long as you live. And whatever you do or whatever happens, remember that."

"Sure thing! Certainly, I mean, Mother," cried the boy, hastily correcting his form of speech at the look in his mother's face. "Seventy times seven is four hundred and ninety, anyway."

The man in the living room picked up the tobacco pouch and retreated softly to his studio. "Seventy times seven—sure thing." The words rang like a bell in his soul. Even if she did come to know, perhaps she too would forgive. He found himself passionately agreeing with the boy. "You're just as good as God," in spite of the blasphemy of it. He went at his work again, closing the door behind him. Somehow the colours were brighter, the light effects more striking, though well he knew that in the background of his mind, as in his picture, there were those deep shadows that no light could pierce. He knew there was hell. He had had a look into its lurid depths within the last twenty-four hours, and he was haunted by the terror that he might know something more of it before long. But "four hundred and ninety times! Seventy times seven! A thousand million times!" Yes, for her innocent little boy. But for him? Still, seventy times seven was four hundred and ninety. He must finish that picture today, and at his work he went with furious zeal. He had never done such good work, and he had come to the finishing touches. He heard Paul planning with his mother for a ride down the valley, perhaps the following day. His heart rose in new hope. She would be well again. But at the very earliest moment he would take her away to the best doctor at Home that money could command. Could she bear the long journey—nearly four thousand miles by land and three thousand by sea? There was that very clever Old Country surgeon in Vancouver everybody was speaking of. Why had he never thought of him? His mind had always gone to the great surgeons of the homeland. But that young McPhail! Why not consult him? He would take her to Vancouver at once. Hour after hour he spent, re-touching the canvas here and there, prancing back and forward with light, eager steps. In his absorption he forgot all but the wonderful scene before him. The door opened softly and his wife entered. He heard nothing.

"Oh, Hugh! how wonderful!" she breathed in ecstasy.

He flung down his brush. "It is finished!" he muttered in an undertone. "And it is good. My best!" He sat looking at it with a detached and critical eye. "Yes, it really is not half bad."

"Half bad!" returned his wife, with indignant scorn. "It ought to be in the Academy!"

"I've seen a lot worse there too," said her husband.

"Of course you have, and few better."

"My dear, you have a wonderful eye! Two of them indeed!" He turned toward her, smiling quizzically.

"Oh, you may smile! But I know pictures a little," she exclaimed defiantly.

"God forbid I should deny it! If you were only on the hanging committee! But, heigh, oh!" he yawned, stretching mightily. "I am fair done. I think I shall take a gun down the valley right after lunch."

"You must be, and you have earned a real holiday. And, Hugh, darling," she came to him with hands lifted,

"I know you finished this just for me." Her face was shining with an inner light, as she locked her hands about his neck.

He stood a moment, looking into her eyes, then gathered her gently into his arms and carried her to a chair, holding her to him.

"Well, I did," he said, his voice a little uncertain. "And," he added, kissing her, "it was worth while."

She settled down into his arms with a little sigh.

"We are very happy, Hugh. I am afraid sometimes we are too happy."

"Too happy? I can 'thole' a lot o' yon," he answered cheerily. "But," he added suddenly, letting into his voice a deeper tone, "as for you, you jolly well deserve all there is going. Now a little rest before lunch, while I get out my gun." He laid her on a lounge, covered her with a wrap and left her, with a smile of pride and ineffable joy illuminating the beauty of her face.

After a hasty lunch Gaspard looked in upon her, found her sleeping quietly and with the adumbration of that same smile still lingering about her, then taking his gun set forth to the completion of the other task he had set himself for the day. A disturbing factor in his day's problem he had learned from old Jinny. Paul had gone off with the Sleeman children, Asa and Adelina, on their ponies for the day, and the boy had spoken of a visit to the Indian camp. Of course, he could send the children off on some chase, but none the less it was a complication which added to the difficulty of a situation sufficiently complex already. He did not, however, anticipate much trouble with Onawata. Her love for him and her native Indian pride would work together to further his purpose. As to the old chief, he was an uncertain and possibly refractory element. A Chippewayan chief of ancient lineage, proud of his race and rank, he had kept his tribe aloof from the life and manners of the white man. He had seen the degradation of other tribes through contact with white civilisation and, following the tradition of his ancestors, he had built up in his people a fear of the white man's power and a contempt for his vices. On the plains of the far north land his people could meet with the white man on equal terms without fear, and at the trading post he could hold his own in shrewd bargaining for the products of trap and gun. He permitted no mingling of blood strains in his tribe, no half-breed could find a home in his wigwams. Next to his passion for his people, his love for his daughter held place with him. Her mother, an Athabascan princess of great beauty and intelligence, trained in one of the out-post Anglican mission schools, had captured his youthful fancy and had held his heart in loyal allegiance for twenty years, until her death twenty-two years ago in giving birth to her only child, Onawata, who, growing up into beautiful girlhood, took her mother's place in her father's heart and became the very light of his eyes, the joy of his heart.

He had not sent her to the mission school. He wanted her kept pure Indian. But he had cleverly cajoled the missionary into setting up among his tribe a kind of extension branch of his school, the principal pupil of which was the chief's daughter. Her extraordinary intelligence, stimulated by her father's ambition for her, enabled her to overcome with remarkable ease and rapidity the initial difficulty of language in acquiring knowledge. She learned to read, to write, to do simple sums, and, not only so, but succeeded in bullying her father into the same knowledge. So that at seventeen she was a sweet, clean, well educated Indian maid of rare intelligence and rarer beauty, the pride of the tribe which she ruled like a queen and the centre and delight of her father's life.

Frankly, Gaspard was afraid to meet the old chief. He relied upon Onawata's influence with him, but it was with very considerable trepidation that he strode into the Indian camp.

A strange scene spread itself before his eyes. On a grassy bench, a little removed from the river bank, were pitched two tents before which were grouped two Indians and at a little distance the chief with his daughter, all intent upon the doings of a group of children and their ponies upon the grass plot before them. The children were dismounted, and their ponies standing, held by their trailing reins, all but Paul, who with the little four-year old Indian child in his arms was galloping up and down the sward to the shrieking delight of the children standing by.

"The Sleeman youngsters and Peg Pelham," he said to himself, as he stood watching. "By Jove! That boy is a rider," he added as his eyes followed the galloping pony with its double load, careering up and down. Almost as he spoke the pony reached the turn, turned on its hind legs and was swinging back on its return trip, when the Sleeman boy sprang forward with a shout, waving his hat. With a quick side jump the pony's feet struck the overhanging cut-bank, broke through, plunged wildly and disappeared, crashing into the underbrush some ten feet below.

Swift as a flash of light, the old chief sprang for the bank, but before him was Gaspard who, clearing the bank with a single leap, was at the head of the struggling pony and, with one hand holding it quiet, grasped with the other the Indian child and, sheltering it with his own body from the kicks of the struggling pony, pulled it clear of danger. It was bravely and cleverly done.

"Paul," he shouted, peering among the underbrush for his son, "where are you?"

"Huh," grunted the chief, whose quick eye had caught sight of the boy farther down the bank, lying motionless at the root of an old birch stump. With one leap the chief was over the pony and at the boy's side. Swiftly he lifted the boy, carried him down to the river's edge and laid him gently down. Then reaching down he scooped up a double handful of water and dashed it into the still, white face. A gasping sob, a shudder of the limbs, and the eyes opened upon the chief's face, then quietly closed again.

"Huh, Kawin! Good!" grunted the chief, whose hands were swiftly moving over the boy's legs and arms. "Good," said the chief again, giving place to the boy's father who had handed over the Indian child to its mother.

"Hello, old boy!" said Gaspard. "All right?"

"All r-i-i-ght," said the boy with a deep sigh. "I'm a-w-f-u-l sle-epy." Gaspard reached down to gather him up in his arms.

"No!" said the chief, placing his hand on Gaspard's arm. "No! Lie down—good. Better soon—five minutes." And Gaspard, kneeling there, waited with white, anxious face. The chief spoke a few words to his daughter who was standing near with her child in her arms. She hurried away and came back in a few moments with a tin cup. The chief took it from her.

"Good," he said with a grunt. "Good. Drink." Gaspard looked at the stuff doubtfully, then at the girl.

"Yes, it is good. The Indians know it is good," she said quietly. Gaspard took the cup and waited till Paul opened his eyes again.

"Here, old chap, drink this," he said, lifting the boy's head.

"My! Daddy, that's awful *a*gusting stuff," he said, screwing up his face.

"Good," said the chief with emphasis. "Drink. Make all better."

"Shall I, Daddy?" said the boy.

"The chief says so, Paul, and he knows."

The boy's eyes went round the circle of faces till they came to the Indian girl's, then rested there. She smiled at him, and took the cup from his father's hand.

"Drink it," she said in a quiet voice. "My little boy drinks it. It will do you good." He drank it up at once.

"Where's Joseph?" he asked suddenly when he had lain some minutes quietly. "He went over too, didn't he?" Joseph was the name of his pinto pony, so called in Scriptural reminiscence of the earliest recorded Joseph, with his coat of many colours.

"He's perfectly all right—clumsy little beggar," said his father.

"And the baby?" said Paul, sitting bolt upright and wide awake.

"He is here and safe," replied the mother. "Your father saved him," she added in a voice that somehow carried a thrilling tone.

"Did you, Daddy? That was fine."

"Pshaw! I just jerked the baby free from Joseph's feet," answered his father almost gruffly.

"Good man! Smart man!" said the chief. "Jump like deer!"

"I guess the angels were smarter'n you, Daddy," observed the boy dreamily.

"Angels? What do you——? Oh, I see," laughed the father.

"Yes, Mother says they just sweep down and keep us from bumping too hard. They do, don't they, Daddy?" enquired the boy, seeking assurance in his father's eyes.

"Why—ah—certainly they do. They got a wing in the way of that old stump sure enough. But are you all right now, old man? Any headache? Arms all right? Legs? Back? All sound, eh?" Paul, moving his various limbs in response to his father's questioning, found them all entire, without bruise or fracture.

They all climbed to the grassy plot above, Paul refusing to be carried, and found waiting them only one little girl, her face showing dead white against the aureole of her bronze-gold hair.

"Hello, Peg," grinned Paul. "Where's Asa and Adelina?"

The little girl, looking very tiny in her riding breeches, gulped very hard once or twice, then rushing at Paul flung herself upon him in a storm of tears.

"Oh, Paul, they said you were dead," she sobbed, clinging to him. "But you're not! You're not!"

"Oh, rot, Peg." Paul cast sheepish eye round the group as he disentangled himself from the clinging arms. "Don't be a silly. What's a fling from a horse? Lots of chaps get that."

The little girl drew away from him, hurt and ashamed, and went slowly toward her pony.

"Where are you going, Peg?" said Paul.

"None of your business," she flung at him, leading her pony toward a convenient stump.

"Peggy!" called Gaspard. Slowly she turned her face toward him. "Peggy, will you do something for me?" He walked over toward her. "Peggy, I want you to take Paul home for me. He is quite all right, I think, but I would feel safer if you were with him. Will you?"

"Yes, Uncle Hugh," said the little girl, her self-respect much restored.

"And, Paul—sure you feel all right?" enquired his father.

"Sure thing. Perfeckly all right, Daddy," replied the boy stoutly.

"Well, then, ride slowly home together. Don't race. And don't tell Mother anything about the accident, about what's happened, till I return. I don't want her frightened. You understand, Paul, don't you? I can trust you, eh?"

"Yes, Daddy, you can trust me." And, sitting his pony very straight and gripping tight with his knees, he set off, crying out, "Good-bye, all! Come along, Peg."

"Good-bye, Uncle Hugh. Good-bye, little baby. Good-bye, all," cried Peg, putting her horse to a gallop to overtake Paul who was just disappearing round a turn in the trail.

CHAPTER VI

When Gaspard turned from waving his son good-bye he found himself facing the chief and his daughter.

"Chief, I want to speak to you about—about—that baby there." He pointed to the child in the girl's arms.

The chief motioned the girl away.

"No, Father, it is my child. I will hear what is said."

"Let her stay," said Gaspard.

The chief grunted acquiescence. Then Gaspard spoke.

"I want to have the boy educated like a white man. I will pay for all. But I want him to live in the North Country with his mother. That is the best place for him just now."

A gleam shot across the haughty face of the old chief.

"Listen!" he said in his own speech, his voice clear and vibrant with passion. "You come to my wigwam, wounded, dying. Our people take you in, bring you back from the land of the Great Spirit. For many moons you live with me, my son, her brother. When you grow strong again you become a wolf, you tear my heart; a thief, you rob my cache of the food on which I live, you take away my treasure, my pride, my honour, my name. On my knees"—he fell on his knees, his face distorted with passion—"I make a prayer to the Great Spirit that some day He will show me your face. That day will wipe out my shame in blood." He rose from his knees. His face once more took on its accustomed look of haughty self-command. "Last night my daughter told me how your woman saved the child from death. Today you too gave your blood for him. I am content. My knife remains in its sheath. I have heard your word. It is not good. The boy is my daughter's son, he is my

56

son. He will be chief after me. He will be Indian. He will learn all that his mother has learned, and more. But he will be Indian. Tomorrow we go to our own land. Never again will we look upon your face, never again will you come to our land. The day you come to our land you will die."

"You will let me pay for the boy's education and—and all that?" Gaspard pleaded in a shaking voice.

"No! No thief shall pay money for the son of Wah-na-ta-hi-ta. Go! dog!"

The tall spare form drawn up to its full height, the out-flung command, the dark eagle-like face, the fiercely blazing eye, the haughty mien, the ringing trumpet tone, all this, with an acute and damnatory consciousness of baseness and all too fully deserved rebuke, combined to produce upon Gaspard's sensitive, artistic soul a truly appalling and overwhelming effect. His whole being shrivelled within him like a growing tree before the blast of a scorching flame. An abasing degradation swept his soul bare of any and every sense of manhood. For some moments he stood utterly deprived of speech or movement. An intolerable agony of humiliation paralysed his mental processes. His mind was blank. He sought for a word but no word seemed adequate. Nor could he move from the spot. Fascinated by that superb, terrible, living embodiment of vengeful judgment, he was held rooted to earth. That final utterance of blighting contempt, "Go! dog!" inhibited thought or motion. Suddenly there flamed up against the blank wall of his imagination, as if in a fiery scroll, the words of ancient doom, "Depart from me, ye cursed." He was conscious at once of an agonising desire to be gone and of an utter powerlessness to lift his feet from their place.

A soft cry and a rush of feet released him. It was Onawata. Swiftly she came to him, flung her arms round his neck, laid her head against his breast, and there rested for a few moments. Then, with her one arm still resting on his shoulder, she faced the old chief and poured forth a passionate defence of the man against whom he had pronounced his bitter and contemptuous indictment. The blame for her wrong was hers as much as his. She had come to him, she had loved him, she loved him still though he had forgotten her. Today he had saved her child from death, and yesterday his woman had done the same. Tomorrow she would depart to her own land, never more would she see his face, but not in humiliation and shame would he leave her now. He would carry with him her heart, her love, her life. While she spoke Gaspard felt a warm tide of gratitude well up within his heart, restoring his manhood, freeing him from the awful sense of abasing degradation which had overwhelmed him the moment before. He passed his arm round the girl and drew her toward him. But even as he did so the Indian girl tore herself free and sprang from him, her eyes staring in horror over his shoulder. Following her eyes, Gaspard turned and there beheld his wife, standing beside her pony, white, silent, bewildered. Slowly she moved toward them.

"Where is Paul?" she asked of her husband. "Is he dead?"

"Dead? Nonsense! He has just gone galloping home with Peg. Who told you about him? He was knocked out a bit, but he is perfectly all right." His words came in a hurried flood, as if he dreaded further questioning.

Standing there, her eyes closed for a moment. "Thank God!" she murmured to herself. Then, opening her eyes as if waking suddenly from sleep, she turned them steadily first on the girl, then on the child, then on her husband and again on the child.

"Hugh, tell me," her voice calm but terrible as the voice of doom, "whose is that child? Remember God hears."

"Mine!" The word leaped forth from the lips of the Indian girl in a shrill cry. "Mine!" she repeated, springing before the man as if to shelter him from attack.

"Hugh, in God's name, tell me truly, whose is that child?"

The man, unnerved by the racking emotions of the last hour and reading in her eyes that she already knew the truth which she dreaded to hear, flung up his hands with a despairing cry.

"God help you, Marion! The child is mine!"

For five full seconds, to him they seemed hours, she stood, white-lipped and staring. Then, turning, she walked with uncertain steps toward her pony, adjusted the reins, attempted to mount, swayed as if to fall, but clutched the mane and hung there.

Gaspard and the girl both sprang to her aid.

"Don't—don't—don't touch me, Hugh!" she gasped, thrusting him from her.

"Marion," he cried, his voice hurried and broken, "let me tell you."

"No, no! Please go." She stood a moment or two, shuddering, her hands over her face as if to shut from her sight a terrible thing, with a choking cry.

"My God, it has come." Gaspard turned from his wife, plunged into the underbrush and was lost to sight.

The Indian woman ran to the other and, clutching her skirt, fell upon her knees crying, "Call him back, call him back quick. Let me call him back. You will lose him forever."

The white woman took her hands from her face, looked down upon the Indian and said in a voice from which all hope had died, "Why call him back? He is lost to me now."

"No, no," said the other, springing to her feet and seizing the white woman's arm. "He is yours, he is yours, only yours. Me! I am nothing to him. It was my fault, my mistake. I knew nothing. I went to him. But to him now I am nothing, nothing. Oh, let me call him back quick." In her vehemence she shook the white woman violently. But to her violence there was no reaction. The wife slowly drew away from the grasp of the Indian woman, climbed somehow on to her pony, and, with the face of one stricken with her death wound, she set off slowly down the homeward trail.

For a single moment the Indian woman followed her with scornful eyes. This supreme, this mad folly in a woman who would turn away from a man who so obviously and so passionately was hers, she could not understand. It was the madness of the white race. White women did not know how to love. She caught up her boy, ran with him to the chief.

"Take him. Keep him till I return," she said fiercely.

"Where do you go?" said the chief sternly.

"I go to save the man I love," she breathed.

"But who loves you not." The chief's tones were eloquent of scorn.

"What matters that? Not for myself I go, but for him. To bring him back—to—her."

"Fool!" said the chief.

"Yes, fool, fool," she answered passionately. "But he will be safe—and—happy." She hurried into her wigwam, snatched a few camp necessities and, swift as a deer, sped on the white man's trail.

CHAPTER VII

For three days the Pine Croft Ranch was plunged in gloom. In her room the lady of the ranch lay, fighting back death till her man should return. She was unwilling to pass out of the world in which together they had shared so deeply of its joys, without another word beyond that last spoken between them.

On the third day Paul, with face pale, tense and worn, rode into the Indian camp to interview the Chief. Straight up he stood, pale, quivering under the nerve strain, but unafraid.

"Mother is very sick," he said. "I'm awful afraid she will die. Father is lost in the woods. She wants him awful bad."

The chief listened, apparently unmoved.

"Mother kept the little baby from dying."

The chief glanced sharply at the little lad. "Huh! I go find him," he said abruptly. He called his men. Together they consulted, apparently canvassing the situation and planning the search. Then, with swift expedition, they prepared for their tramp. In a very few minutes the chief and one of his men stood ready for their journey, the other man remaining in camp with the child. Before setting forth, the chief came to the boy.

"You go mother," he said. "Good woman! Two day father he come back. Sure, two day. Tell mother. Good woman. Chief not forget baby."

"Oh, thank you, Chief," said the little boy, impulsively catching his hand. "I'll tell Mother. She will be awfully thankful to you. Good-bye. Everything will be right now."

"Huh!" grunted the chief, and with a wave of the hand he was gone.

"Hello, little one," Paul called, catching sight of the Indian child standing shyly within the tent door. "Come on over here. Come on and see my pony."

The child, with a fearlessness quite unusual among Indian children, came trotting to him. Paul was delighted to find he was not forgotten.

"I say, little chap, tell me your name again," he said, dropping on his knees beside the youngster. The little chap gurgled a reply. "What is it?" Again a gurgle. Paul gave an answering gurgle. "Is that it?"

The stolid face of the Indian standing near suddenly broke into a grin.

"Him name Peter," he said with a struggle.

"Peter," shouted the boy, with a delighted laugh. "And I'm Paul. Oh, isn't that funny? Peter and Paul! Why, we are two Apostles." He caught up the little child and danced about with him in high glee, and the glee of the little one was no less high. Then for half an hour the grave-faced Indian looked upon a scene that more than once broke up his gravity. For with all sorts of games and antics the white boy tumbled the other about upon the grass, driving him into shrieks of delighted laughter, such as in his rather sombre four years of life in the wigwam with his stolid seniors he had never been known to utter. In the full tide of his play Paul remembered his duty.

"Here, Peter, old chap, I must get away home," he cried, rolling off from his back the little Indian who had been using him as a pony. "Good-bye. I'll see you again soon."

But a fierce howl of protest brought him back running. It was only after he had emptied his pockets of his treasures, a top, a knife, some peppermints, somewhat the worse for wear but none the less toothsome to Peter, impervious to the microbe terror, that he was able to make his escape in an atmosphere of smiling serenity.

"Two days!" The chief's promise he knew would be kept. In two days his father, whose mysterious absence had wrought such havoc in the life of home, would be back again, and then the old serene and happy life would be restored. In two days that dreadful fear which had been clutching at his heart all yesterday and this morning and which the memory of his mother's face even now brought back to him would be gone. Two days! He let his pony out to his full speed, eager to bring the great news to his mother.

.   .   .   .

Two days later the chief appeared at the bungalow, supporting a stumbling, ragged, half-starved man who fell sprawling at the steps and lay there waiting for strength to make the ascent. The chief passed quickly into the living room and finding no one went on into the kitchen. There he found old Jinny, rocking in her arms a haggard, grief-distracted boy who sobbed in his sleep. The old nurse, catching sight of the chief, held up her hand for silence.

"Man come! Drink!" muttered the Indian, picking up a cup from the table and going through the motion of drinking. Old Jinny, nodding comprehension, rose with the boy in her arms, carried him to a sofa and laying him gently down turned to the Indian with her finger on her lips, then passing into the living room procured a glass of liquor and gave it to the Indian.

"Come," he ordered, and she followed promptly and without a word. Together they lifted the exhausted Gaspard, gave him the drink, and waited till his strength should come back.

"The Lord help the man, he maun dree his weird! It's a sair warl for him." Then, turning to the chief who stood as if cut from stone, she said:

"Gae awa', you, tae Colonel Pelham," she commanded him, "tae the big white hoose doon the way yonder, and tell him the woman's deid." But her speech was beyond the Indian till, baffled, she beckoned him into the house.

"Come," she said, and took him into the room where

the dead woman lay. At once the chief understood. Down the driveway she went with him and pointed the way to the "big white house" of Colonel Pelham. Without a word he was off on his errand, on the long swinging trot of the Indian, while the old nurse returned to the man who still lay upon the steps, too spent to move. She bent over him, shook him awake, and said, "Come, man, get ye in till y're bed. Ye're no fit for onything." He turned dull eyes upon the house.

"Jinny," he mumbled, "my—your—Marion—she is better?"

"Aye, she's better," said the old nurse calmly. "She's beyond all ill." Jinny was entirely preoccupied with grief over the death of the woman she had nursed as a babe and whose babes she had nursed as well.

The man staggered to his feet and held by the verandah post, struggling for breath.

"Jinny," he gasped. "No—no—you don't—mean —she's——" He could get no further.

"Aye, she's deid. Gude save us a', my sweet lassie is deid." The old woman threw her apron over her head and burst into wailing. "Aye, the puir lassie, the puir lassie! Ma bonnie wee lamb! She's awa', she's awa'."

The man stared stupidly upon the rocking, wailing figure at his feet.

"Dead! Dead!" he said in a harsh voice. "It's a lie. It's a lie! She wouldn't die that way. She wouldn't die without a word to me."

"Aye, she left ye a word as she was bleedin' ta deith. A pail full o' bluid she pit up. Wae's me! But she didna forget ye." Old Jinny's voice took a grudging note. "She left ye a word." She went into the house, returning in a minute with a torn piece of paper. Gaspard took it with a shaking hand, dropped it with a cry.

"What's that on it?" he gasped pointing at a stain upon the white paper. "What's that? You old—fool— don't tell me it's——" His voice became a shriek. "My

God—my God! It's blood! Her blood!" He pointed at the stained paper a finger that wavered and shook, his face white, his eyes fierce and glaring like those of a mad man.

"Aye, it's her bluid. The blessed lamb!" said Jinny picking up the paper. "She pit her dyin' lips till it—the bluid——"

"Stop! Stop! For Heaven's sake, stop! Do you want to kill me?" cried the man, his voice shrill, strident, broken.

"Oh, Daddy, Daddy! You're here! Oh, I'm glad you're here!" The child's voice rang out in a cry of wild joy. In the doorway he paused, looking from one to the other, then flung himself at his father.

Gaspard made as if to thrust him off, but on a second impulse he gathered the boy in his arms and sank down, moaning, on the steps.

"She's gone, she's gone! Oh, God, let me go! Let me go too! She's left us, boy! She's left us!"

"Yes, Daddy," said the boy quietly, his hand reaching up to his father's cheek. "And she said you would go and me too, Daddy. I want to go with you, Daddy."

His father only groaned.

"And she made me promise to tell you about my very last lesson." Still the father was silent, heedless of the boy's talk. "My Bible lesson, you know, Daddy. She made me promise to tell you about it. Are you listening, Daddy?"

"What! Oh, yes, yes, go on boy. What was it you were saying?" His father roused himself to listen.

"She made me promise to tell you my lesson."

"Yes! Go on!"

"About the seventy times seven, you remember."

"Seventy times seven?" The man was broad awake.

"Yes, you know, seventy times seven in one day. That's four hundred and ninety times in one day we must forgive. And she said, 'Be sure, be very sure to tell Daddy that.' She said you would be awful glad to hear that. Why, Daddy? And she said it was the lesson she loved best in all the Bible. I don't think so, do you Daddy?"

"Seventy times seven! She said that. Oh, my God, my God! Seventy times seven! Seventy times seven!" Convulsive, mighty sobs shook his great body. The boy was terrified, too terrified to speak. His father's eyes fell upon the stained bit of paper, lying where it had fallen from his fingers. Shuddering, he picked it up. There in poor wandering letters he read:

"My dear, dear love—I want you so—oh—I want you so. I want to ask you to forgive—to tell you—oh, I want you—with me—now—dear heart——" Then one desperate trailing scrawl as if death were clutching at her fingers. "Remember—70 × 7——" Then a poor faltering "X" and the marks of blood. "She pit her dyin' lips till it," old Jinny had said.

With an agonising cry he put the boy from him, scrambled up the steps, staggered through the living room, felt his way blindly into the bedroom where she lay. One glance he gave at the white still face touched with the calm dignity of death. Then with a bitter cry he fell on his knees at the bedside, gathered the quiet form in his arms, and there drank slowly, drop by drop, to the last dregs, the cup of his Gethsemane.

Terrified, petrified with his terror, his little son stood behind him, his limbs shaking under him, impotent of motion, desperately longing but unable to escape from the room, till at length, overcome by the tumultuous tide of his emotions, with a sobbing cry, "Oh, Daddy, I'm afraid," he flung himself on his knees at his father's side and there clung to him.

In that position the wife of Colonel Pelham found them half an hour later.

"Paul, dear, come with me," she said, trying to lift him up.

"I want Daddy," whispered the boy, still clinging to his father.

"Mr. Gaspard," she said sharply, "this boy must be put to bed at once. He will be ill."

The man raised his face, ghastly, unshaven, horrible.

"What do you say?" he asked dully.

"The boy, the boy," she said, pointing to him. "He ought to be in bed. He will be ill."

"Yes, yes," he said stupidly. "Certainly, he must go to bed. Come, Paul." He rose to his feet, and with the boy in his arms staggered into the living rooom, stood there, swaying drunkenly, and would have fallen had not Colonel Pelham caught him and steadied him to a couch where he lay moaning, "Gone, gone, gone! Oh, my God! Gone forever!" till from sheer weakness, due to starvation and emotional exhaustion, he sank into deathlike sleep.

The boy crept in beside him, stroking his cheek and whispering, "Poor Daddy! Poor Daddy!" till he too fell asleep.

CHAPTER VIII

The "big white house" was overflowing with music, or, rather, with musical acrobatics. Scales, major and minor, octaves, arpeggios, and all other musical combinations were madly chasing each other up and down the keyboard.

"Come on, Paul." A girl's black head appeared at the window. The player merely glanced at her and went on with his fireworks. "Oh, come on, you lummix! Shut up this row and come on. We're going round the ranch and then down the west trail to the river."

The player's sole answer was a wave of his left hand, his right still careering madly up the chromatic scale.

"Aw, Paul, won't you come?" A little girl whose face was screwed up in a bewitching pout came to the door.

"Now, Peg, you know I don't quit till I'm done, and I've got half an hour yet. Come back for me then, Peg."

She came close to him. "I don't want to go with Asa and Adelina without you. They—they—I don't want to go."

"Oh, go on, Peg, for a run as far as Pine Croft driveway and back again. Go! See, the rain is all gone. It's a lovely day. Run now, that's a good girl. I'll come when I'm through my practice."

"You're a mean old thing. You don't care a bit about me," said Peg, bouncing indignantly out of the room.

But the boy paid no heed. He was hard at his scales again with an enthusiasm which amounted almost to a passion. All else, for the time being, was as nothing to him. He was at double octaves now, his fingers roaring up and down the keys. In the full tide of the uproar Colonel Pelham appeared at the door of the dining room where his wife was engaged in her domestic activities.

"What a row the chap makes!" he said. "You'd think it was a full grown man at the thing."

"He has wonderful fingers," said his wife, pausing in her work. "Listen! Now, that is really quite unusual work."

"Is it? You ought to know. It's all fury and fuss to me. But I like the way he sticks it. The other youngsters were trying to pull him away—I saw them at it, but it was no go."

"He loves his music. He's quite mad about it," replied his wife.

"He may be," said the Colonel, "but it's not that. It's a point of honour with him. He has a kind of feeling his mother would like it."

"He's a queer little chap, you know. He has queer ideas about things."

"What do you mean exactly?" inquired the Colonel. "Queer in what sense?"

"Well," said his wife thoughtfully, "he has queer ideas about God. He says he sees Him. One day I found him with an intense look upon his face, and his explanation was that he was listening for God."

" 'Speak, Lord, for Thy servant heareth,' " quoted the Colonel to himself.

"But, my dear," protested his wife, "you know that sort of thing was quite all right for those times. But now-a-days, in British Columbia—well, you know, it's a little unusual."

" 'If any man hear My voice and open the door,' " again quoted the Colonel softly.

"Oh, come now, Edgar. You don't think those things are to be taken literally in these days—voices, and all that sort of thing. You'll be off into all sorts of Spiritualistic nonsense. He *is* queer. As a matter of fact, he is almost uncanny, unreal, unnatural."

"Unnatural? Unreal? Well, he is a bit of a mystic, I confess. And he came by that naturally enough; got it from his mother. And not a bad thing, either, in these materialistic days, and in this country. But all the same, he's a real boy, a game sport. He can ride, swim, shoot, and for a boy of twelve shows an extraordinary sense of responsibility."

"Responsibility? He's as mad as a March hare at times," said the Colonel's wife. "Forgets food, drink, sleep. He has appalling powers of absorption, of concentration. I know he leads Peg into all sorts of scrapes."

"Leads Peg!" exclaimed her husband. "Good Lord! Does any one lead Peg? He's a real boy, he gets into scrapes, but I still contend that he has an extraordinary sense of responsibility. Do you realise that every day of his life he has a certain routine of study, music, Catechism, Bible lesson, and that sort of thing, that he has kept up since his father left him? I believe it was his father—a queer thing too!—who put it up to him and who made it a matter of loyalty to his mother."

"He is certainly devoted to his mother's memory. But there again he is queer. He has an idea that his mother knows, hears, understands all that he does."

"Why not?" asked the Colonel.

"Oh, I don't know. I have no use for these spooky things. But the boy is queer, and he is unpractical."

"Well, it is hardly to be wondered at. He has his father's artistic temperament and his mother's mysticism. But, after all, is he unpractical? Don't you know that once a week, winter and summer, for the last year and a half, with Indian Tom he has ridden the marches of the ranch? The Lord knows he's always reporting fences broken and cattle and horses straying over to Sleeman's herd," added the Colonel ruefully.

"Sleeman's herd! My opinion is that the chronic state of disrepair in those fences can be easily accounted for. I observe that Sleeman's calves last year and this year too show a strong Saddle-back strain, and as for his colts they are all Percheron. I don't like the man Sleeman. I don't trust him."

"Neither does Paul," said the Colonel. "Of course,

Paul has quite made up his mind that Sleeman is going to hell, so he doesn't let his various iniquities worry him too much. Sleeman will receive a due reward for his misdeeds. Paul has warmly adopted the Psalmist's retribution point of view."

"What do you mean?" inquired his wife.

" 'Fret not thyself because of evil doers, for they shall soon be cut down like the grass and wither as the green herb.' The little beggar brought me the quotation not long ago with great satisfaction. He thinks that Asa too is heading toward the same untimely end."

"Why!" said his wife, "I thought that Paul held a most liberal doctrine of forgiveness, which practically wiped out hell."

"Don't imagine any such thing," asserted her husband. "I know his 'seventy times seven' theory, but he is careful to insist that this is only for the man who turns and repents. He would be terribly disappointed, I imagine, if Sleeman should ever show any signs of repentance. Of course, he doesn't expect this. Oh, he's a relentless little devil in his hatred and his theories of judgment. And with a fighting strain in him, too."

"What do you mean?" asked his wife. "Fighting?"

"Why, you remember last autumn when he came to me with the calm request that I teach him to fight. He had evidently had some trouble with Asa. When I asked him why he wanted to learn to fight, his answer was characteristic enough, 'I don't want to fight exactly,' he said, 'but I don't want to feel afraid to fight.' Rather a fine distinction, I think. And every week since that time the little beggar insists upon his 'fighting' lesson."

"Well," said his wife with a slight smile, "he couldn't have come to a better master of the art, I fancy, if college rumours mean anything. Wasn't it light-weight championship you held for a year at Oxford?"

"Three years, my dear," modestly corrected the Colonel.

"There is one thing I do like in the boy," continued

Mrs. Pelham, "and that is his devotion to old Jinny. Of course, Jinny worships the ground he walks on. She has all that fine old Scotch spirit of devotion and loyalty to the family that this age and this country know nothing about. She is an old dear, and immensely helpful about the house. But I do like Paul's way with her. I always say that there is no truer sign of breeding than the way people treat their servants, and Paul certainly has that fine touch."

In a pause of the conversation weird sounds were heard coming from the music room. The musical acrobatics had ceased. Both sat listening for some moments.

"Now what is he on?" the Colonel inquired. "I don't know that thing."

"Nor I, and I've looked over all his father's things which he is continually trying. Listen! Sounds like a Chopin Nocturne. But, no! That's not Chopin. He must be improvising. He told me one day he was playing all the things out of doors, a kind of Nature Symphony, the Pine Croft out of doors, as it were—the stream tumbling down beside the bungalow, the pines and the poplars and the flowers and the clouds. He told me he was playing the great yellow splashes of sunlight on the valley. He kept me an hour that day, fascinated, playing the different colours in the landscape—blue of the sky, light, sweet, smooth-flowing, a Handel sort of thing; reds and yellows were set forth in dashing, smashing chords and runs, a Liszt or Tschaikowsky effect; then, for sunset gold and saffron he used a kind of Mozart thing, rich, full, sweet. It was quite marvellous. He is queer, undoubtedly queer. Why! Do you know he had the audacity to even play 'God' to me that day. He was like an inspired thing. Played 'God smiling at him from the clouds.' He protests he sees God, you know, and hears Him. Oh, he's quite spooky!"

"Spooky? Nonsense! That's not the word. There are artistic and mystic strains in him, that's all. But all the same, I wonder when his father is coming back, or if he is coming back at all. That Pine Croft Ranch is going bad. I simply can't keep it on."

"Of course you can't. You were mad to take it on at first."

"My dear Augusta, what could I do? The man was distracted, broken. I was actually afraid for his brain. I really was. You remember those days. Well—then came his request and the formal will—by Jove! Now I think of it, it was you who offered to take the boy."

"The boy? Yes, I did. But the ranch was a different thing. And that Sleeman sniffing round, I simply can't bear him."

"Sleeman? I don't much care for him myself. He may be honest enough, but he's sharp. Says he holds I O U's for loans and such like from Gaspard. True enough, Gaspard was hard up. You know the Bank had closed down on him. He could get no more extensions. Frankly, I am worried. The stock is running wild, as you say."

"Edgar, I forbid you to worry. It's not worth it. We'll look after the boy. The bungalow is closed up, everything all right there; old Tom looks after it. The ranch and stock must simply take care of themselves."

At this point a louder crash than usual on the piano arrested their attention. A wild whoop followed, and Paul stood in the doorway.

"Oh, Uncle Colonel, where are they? Did you see them go?" he burst forth.

"Come, Paul," said the Colonel's lady severely. "It's not customary to rush in upon people like that." The boy flushed to his hair roots.

"I'm sorry, Aunt Augusta. Awfully sorry, Uncle Colonel. But did you see them go, sir?"

"Yes, they went up toward Pine Croft Ranch. But you ought to be able to track them easily, for the rain has softened the trail."

"Oh, splendid! I'll do it. I'll just get Joseph and find them."

"By the way, what were you playing last, Paul?" asked the Colonel. The boy flushed.

"Oh, just some nonsense, Uncle Colonel. I was through with my lesson," he said apologetically, "and I was just fooling a bit—like Daddy used to do sometimes—" he paused, "for Mother and me, you know." He stood quietly, looking out the door, his eyes on the far mountains.

"All right, boy. Off you go," said the Colonel.

"Lunch at one, Paul, remember," said Mrs. Pelham.

"I'll try, Aunt Augusta. But it's awfully hard to remember sometimes."

"I want Peg at one," said Mrs. Pelham firmly. "We have something on after lunch. I depend upon you, Paul."

"Oh, all right, then, I'll have to remember." He stuck his hand in his pocket and extracted something which he began to wind around his finger.

"What's that, old chap? String, eh?"

"A 'lastic band—to remember me about one o'clock. I hate having to remember," he added impatiently.

"Hey day!" exclaimed Mrs. Pelham. "What sort of a boy would you be if you couldn't remember?"

"All right, Aunt Augusta, but I hate it all the same."

"He'll remember," said the Colonel. "He feels he's on his honour."

"Yes, he'll remember. He's a reliable little beggar."

In a surprisingly short time the lad appeared on his pony, a beautiful pinto, bred from an Arabian sire out of an Indian pony, a strain of which his father was inordinately proud and in the breeding of which he had been unusually successful. The boy went flashing past the window, riding cowboy fashion, straight leg and with lines held loosely in his left hand, his cap high in his right, making right for the bars at the end of the drive.

"What the—— By Jove, he's done it! Must be quite four feet."

With never a halt the pony had taken the bars in his

stride, and was off down the road, head down and at racing speed.

"Superb, Augusta! Couldn't have done it better yourself, what?"

"He can ride," said his wife. Her eyes were upon the flying figure. "He is quite without fear and has the true rider's instinct for what his mount can do. Wonderful pony of his that. There's a mate to it in Gaspard's bunch I'd like for Peg."

"Oh, thanks, my dear; Peggy is quite sufficiently well mounted. Tubby does her quite well. I have no desire to see my daughter tearing like a mad thing after that race horse."

"Poor old Tubby! She does her best, but I fear she is a continual source of humiliation and heartache to her rider when out with the pinto. Perhaps next year, eh? She will be quite ready to ride with me by that time."

"With you? The Lord forbid! You know quite well, my dear, when once you are astride a horse you are conscious only of one consuming passion."

"Well, I like to hear you talk!" And it must be confessed there was ground for her scorn. For in cross-country work in the Homeland there was just one place in the hunt that gave any real satisfaction to the little Colonel, as daring a hunter as ever rode to hounds.

Meantime the pinto and his rider had tracked the others up to the Pine Croft bungalow, along the upper trail, and down again toward the big rapid. To Paul, who for the past two years had been trained in sign reading by Indian Tom, his father's ancient factotum, the trail lay plain as the open road. After the first wild gallop he was in no hurry to catch up. The glory of the early June day filled his world, right up to the blue sky. With his eyes open to the unending variety of colour and form in the growing things about him, he cantered slowly along, his lithe form swaying in unison with every motion of his pony. He had the make of a rider and his style was a curious mixture of his father's and Indian Tom's. His

hands were his father's; the easy yielding sway of his
body he had from Indian Tom. But, whatever its
source, every movement of every part of his body was
smooth, easy, graceful. As the pinto carried him along
in swallow-like movement, his mind following his eye
went first to the pictures that kept composing and dis-
solving themselves on either side, and from them to those
pictures which from his earliest years he had watched
his father call into being in his studio. Where was his
father now? For three years there had been silence,
from that dreadful day when his father, gaunt, broken,
his great frame heaving with deep-drawn sobs, had ridden
down the Golden trail, followed by Indian Tom, leaving
him with Colonel Pelham. Two words only had his
father spoken, two unforgettable words. "Paul, your
mother has gone to God. Let every morning bring back
to you her words." And the other, "Some day I will
come back to you—point of honour," using a phrase
common to those three when the word was pledged. Those
two words he carried in his heart. With every opening dawn his first thoughts went to his mother. He was
dismayed to find how few were his mother's words that
came to him as he sat down deliberately to recall them.
To his delight he stumbled upon a plan. When struggling
with his Catechism—it was a point of honour that he
should complete the task his mother had not seen completed—he found upon reviewing the questions he had
discussed with her that floods of memories were let loose
upon his mind. With painful care, for, though he had
his father's fingers and was clever with them, he had
made no very great progress with his penmanship, he
undertook to set down, in one of his father's sketch books,
all her sayings that came back to him. The words associated with the Bible stories were much easier to recall.
The chirography and orthography would have quite
paralysed the intelligence of learned experts, but to himself the record was perfectly intelligible, and with its
increasing volume became an increasingly precious pos-

session. This record he kept hidden from mortal eyes, but somehow he had the conviction both God and his mother knew all about it. The two were very really and vitally associated in his thought. Indeed, God had come nearer since his mother had passed out of his sight. His mother, he knew, was intimately involved in his life, sharing his thoughts, his imaginations, his dreams. And since she had gone to God, naturally it followed that God must be somehow, somewhere, quite close at hand. He no longer saw God's face up in the blue between the clouds. He was deeply grieved that he never could visualise that kindly face looking down, so quiet and so kind, "as if He liked him." It seemed as if God had moved much nearer to him, so near that he seemed to be aware of Him, and by intently "listening with his ears inside," as he explained to Indian Tom who seemed to quite understand, he could "hear God thinking." "And so," as he confidently asserted to the gravely sympathetic Indian, "I always know what He wants me to know." Life was a very simple proceeding with Paul. He had only to listen carefully and, having heard, to give heed.

But where was his father, and when would he come back? The little Colonel was quite silent upon that question, and upon that question the boy was equally reserved with the Colonel. With a maturity ripened by responsibility, the boy had fallen into the habit of keeping an eye upon the ranch matters. His own observation was quickened by the rare but penetrating comments of Indian Tom who, though deficient in initiative and inclined when not impelled to activity by necessity, to a *laissez faire* attitude towards life, was nevertheless, when once set upon a trail, tenacious of his quest as a bloodhound on the scent. It was a remark of Indian Tom's that gave the Colonel's lady the clue as to Sleeman's Saddle-backs and Percherons. It was a grunt of Indian Tom's that had set Paul off one day on a tour round the ranch, and that first tour with Indian Tom proved so fascinating that once a week for a year and a half, through rain or shine, cold or heat, Paul had ridden round the line of fences of the ranch. He had come to know that things were not going well, and this knowledge intensified in him the longing for his father's return.

The sound of shouting broke the current of his thoughts. He pulled up his pony and stood listening. "They're away beyond the big rapid," he said to himself. "Must be down by the creek." Again the shouting came to him, and in an instant he was off at a gallop. A short run brought him to the edge of a rapidly flowing stream along which a cow path ran. Following this path he came upon an open grassy meadow through which the stream had cut its way between overhanging banks. At a little distance he saw his friends, and as he drew near learned the cause of the shouting. The stream had cut a channel about eight feet wide, through which the water ran, deep and swift, to a pool some thirty yards farther down, from which it tumbled over jagged rocks to a bench below. Across this flowing stream Asa and his sister were jumping their horses in high glee, and taunting Peg to attempt the same exploit.

"Hurrah! Out of the way there!" shouted Paul, heading his pony toward the jump. With his ears pricked forward the pinto approached the stream on an easy lope. "Up there, old chap," cried Paul, lifting his pony with the reins. With never a pause, the pony gathered himself in two or three quick strides and went sailing over the stream like a bird.

"That's nothing," cried Asa, a stocky youth of fourteen, mounted on a fine rangy cow pony. "Watch old Kicker do it." He took his broncho back a few yards and at racing speed cleared the stream with ease.

"That's the way we do it, eh?" he shouted back at the others.

"Aw, pshaw! Who couldn't do that?" cried Paul scornfully.

"*She* can't! She's afraid!" jeered Asa, pointing to

sitting quietly on the fat and placid Tubby,
g gloomily upon the swift-flowing water.

on Peg," called Asa, "if old Tubby can't jump
at acrost."

se she can jump it if she wants to," said Paul,
n in the whole situation. "But Peg needn't
doesn't want to." As he spoke he circled
e pinto and once more cleared the stream.

ren't. She's afraid." Asa's laugh made Peg

t afraid to jump, but I don't think Tubby wants
she said to Paul. Asa shouted.

me acrost as easy as anything," said Adelina
"An' I kin do it again."

course you did. An' yeh kin do it again any ole
yeh want to," said her brother.

aul's glance wandered from one girl to the other.
eg's face was pale and set. She was the youngest of
the party, tall for her age, but slight in body and of a
highly nervous and sensitive temperament. Asa's taunting jeers disturbed her but little, but Adelina's smooth
superior tone stung her like the lash of a whip. Her pale
face flushed a bright red.

"I'm *not* afraid, and I can do it if I want to," she
said with quick defiance.

"Go it then! Let's see you!" cried Asa.

"Don't you do it, Peg, if you don't want to," said
Paul quietly. "Never mind him!"

"Here, young feller, you keep y're mouth shut," said
Asa truculently, rushing his broncho at Paul.

"I'm going to do it," said Peg, as Paul swerved his
pinto out of Asa's way.

"Don't try it, Peg," said Adelina's smooth voice. "You
know old Tubby's pretty slow, an' she might fall in."
The insult was more than Peg could bear, to whom Tubby
was a friend greatly beloved.

"I'm going, Paul," said Peg, between her shut teeth.

"All right, Peg, I'll go with you. Come on, we'll take

it together." As he spoke they took their p⟨
and went at the jump full gallop.

"Hai-yai!" yelled Asa, as, thundering dow⟨
from behind, he put his broncho between th⟨
Whether it was the sudden yell that cause⟨
Tubby to lose her stride, or whether it wa⟨
rush of the broncho's feet behind her that m⟨
her nerve, as Tubby rose for the leap Peg ⟨
and next instant Tubby was floundering in ⟨
running water and Peg floating down to⟨
pool.

"Swim, Peg," shouted Asa, rather alarmed at t⟨
springing from his broncho and running toward th⟨
But poor Peggy's swimming powers, at best of the⟨
est, were more than neutralised by the shock and ⟨
of her sudden plunge, and it was all she could do to ⟨
afloat while she was being swept down toward the p⟨
and the rocks below. The roar and splash of the rapids⟨
struck terror to her heart.

"Oh, Paul, save me!" she shrieked, beginning to splash
wildly.

"All right, Peg, I'll get you," cried Paul. Like a flash
he swung his pony on its heels, dashed down the stream
and plunged into the pool. As the water came up over
the saddle he slipped off, holding to the stirrup. "Here
you are, Peg," he shouted, as the pony headed off the
floating girl from the rapid. Reaching out, he seized her
dress and held firm, while Joseph gallantly made for the
farther bank and clambered up to safety, Tubby meantime managing to scramble out of danger.

"All right, Peg, eh?" gasped Paul, holding the child
close to him.

"Oh, Paul," cried Peg, crying and choking. "It wasn't
—Tubby's—fault. I pulled her."

"No! It wasn't Tubby's fault, nor your fault. It was
that—that—that—damn beast, Asa," pointing across the
stream to the bigger boy who stood, white and shaken,
beside his sister. "I don't care, I've said it and I mean

He's a damn, damn, damn beast!

himself with fury. "And I don't
pent. It's true! And God doesn't
ruth, and he is a beast and a damn
o hell, I know. And he just de-
ask God to send him there."

Peg in sobbing delight. "I think

y in a gruff voice, pulling off his
ry. "Put this on and let us get
rly one, and I promised."
he coat. The warm June sun soon
nts steaming. Paul caught Tubby,
swung himself on Joseph and with
thers across the stream rode off at
e o'clock appointment. For a full
nto have his head, to the great and
Tubby, heroically resolved not to
ly he pulled up and waited for

be awful mad," he growled.
Peg serenely. Already she was
which would follow her tale. "Oh,
mad, weren't you?" said Peg with
the memory of Paul's terrible out-
used such dreadful words in all his
the provocation. Indeed, she had
tingly predict Asa's post mortem
dulgence in that very same sort of

d Paul rudely. "It was all your

l," replied Peg sweetly. She under-
Paul meant, and she was not a little
been the occasion of Paul's moral
f which was but the measure of his
was never quite sure of her standing

with Paul when Adelina was a
much stronger and braver and c
things that boys could do.   Too
silent agonies of jealousy and h
evident admiration of Adelina's n
Today she was quite sure that
flung himself headlong from his
tude for Adelina's sake.   Her mo
her," might indeed punish her.
exaltation she felt she would en
glanced at her face, puzzled not
serenity, and all the more deeply
serenity.

"It was your fault," he repeated
have to repent—or go to hell.   A
pent.   I just hate to."

"Oh, never mind, Paul," comf
think God will care about Asa.
and he's going to hell anyway, you

But this view of the matter bro
Not but that he was quite clear i
destiny, but he was equally clear
up his feeling of righteous indigna
in very truth before he went to sle
have to repent, a thought most di
turned wrathfully upon his compar

"Much you know about it," he
disdaining further conversation wit
at a gallop, lest he should fail of
honour" engagement.

The meeting with Aunt August
great concern to Peg, was fraught t
amount of anxiety.   It was an ac
standing that on these excursions
charge and for her he must assume
means an insignificant burden, as
more occasions than one.   He had
to escape trouble.   There was no esc

penetration, and to do him justice it never occurred to Paul to attempt to do so. He was fully prepared to accept the full consequences of the escapade. A greater burden, however, weighed down his spirits, the burden of his moral delinquency. For the ordinary sins of his daily life, the way to forgiveness and to consequent restoration of his peace and of his self-respect was quite plain. The removal of this sin, however, by the simple method of repentance and forgiveness was complicated by new and perplexing elements. It was a grave complication, for instance, that repentance was an antecedent condition to forgiveness. He was at present conscious of no regret for his language. Back in the shadows of his mind he knew there lurked a secret and distinctly pleasurable satisfaction in recalling the phrase in which he had described the boy who had undoubtedly acted in a thoroughly beastly fashion. The phrase he had used continued, even while violating his sense of rectitude, to give him a thrill of unholy joy. How could he repent of that phrase which he felt to be at once true and wholly adequate? Then, too, the pathway to pardon was hedged by the condition of his forgiving Asa. In his mood that was hopelessly impossible.

Before he had reached a solution of these moral and theological problems, they had arrived at Peg's home. At the door they were welcomed by Peg's mother.

"Why, Peggy!" she exclaimed. "What do you mean by wearing Paul's coat a hot day like this?"

"Oh, Mamma," cried Peg, her voice vibrant with excitement, "Paul put it on me to keep me from taking cold."

"Taking cold, child? Why should you take cold? Here, let me see you." She pulled the coat off the little girl and discovered her soaked condition. "Why, good heavens! What has happened to you? Where have you been? What does this mean, Paul?" she added severely, turning to Paul.

"She fell into the creek, Aunt Augusta. We were jumping our horses across, and Tubby slipped and fell in."

"Oh, Mamma—" began Peg in high excitement.

"It was our fault, Aunt Augusta," cut in Paul, meantime scowling heavily at Peg, hoping to check the exuberance of her recital. "Asa and I were jumping our horses across the stream, and Peggy tried and Tubby fell in."

"Well, you ought to have known better, Paul. I trust Peggy to you, and you ought to take better care of her."

"I know, Aunt Augusta, and—and—and I'm awfully sorry."

"You have a right to be sorry," said Aunt Augusta indignantly. "Well, get your horses away and come in to lunch. And take off those wet things. Come away, Peg. You are a foolish little thing."

When Paul returned to the house after rubbing down the ponies and turning them loose in the paddock, he found Aunt Augusta's mood quite changed, and he knew that Peggy must have told the whole story. Whether her recital had covered the story of his moral collapse remained an anxious uncertainty in his mind. He could only await developments.

"Come here, boy," said the Colonel, as Paul entered the room. "You are a plucky little chap, and I want to tell you that I shan't forget what you did for Peg today." The little Colonel's voice grew suddenly husky. He shook Paul warmly by the hand and turned away, leaving Paul standing overwhelmed with embarrassment and filled with rage at Peggy. But an even more trying experience awaited the unhappy Paul, when Aunt Augusta came to him and, putting her arms around him, drew him close and kissed him, a most unusual proceeding with her.

"Paul," she said, "I am sorry I spoke to you as I did. And I am glad it was not your fault. I know I can trust Peggy with you always. Now, come away to lunch."

Paul found himself gulping and fighting hard to keep back the tears, tears caused partly by Aunt Augusta's unusual demonstration of affection and partly by his furious indignation at Peg, that she should have given him away. It did not help matters much that Peg insisted during the lunch hour of reiterating her various thrilling experiences, her emotions of fear and despair and relief and joy, her admiration of Paul's heroic courage, her gratitude, and all the rest of it. Paul was grateful, however, that apparently up to this point Peg had so far observed the decencies as to make no reference to his lamentable "fall from grace."

Immediately after lunch, with the timely assistance of Aunt Augusta, who seized upon Peg and promptly put her to bed, Paul was able to effect his escape from the household, and betook himself to the solitude of Pine Croft Ranch. There, under the pines on the hill at the back of the bungalow, which had become to him a holy place, a very temple of God, where he was wont to hold his secret communions with his own spirit and with the world unseen, he entered upon the soul conflict which had to be fought out before he could sleep in peace.

How it came he could not tell, but somehow, before the pines at the far horizon across the river had cast their long lance-shaped shadows upon the plain below, he had found his way to peace. As he lay upon his back, looking up through the waving tops of the great pine trees into the blue of the sky above, the surging tides of furious rage against Asa and his sense of ill-desert which had deepened within him throughout the early afternoon faded, in some mysterious way, from his soul, as the mists before the rising sun. There, beneath the pines, he became aware of a mighty Presence, comforting, cleansing, healing, that made all else seem insignificant. He was his own man again, and once more in tune with those vast infinities in the midst of which he moved and had his being. Chastened and at peace with himself and all his world, he returned to the big white house, ready to meet with a serene heart whatever life might bring to him.

It was well that it was so, for the morrow had in store for him experiences that should test to the uttermost the quality of that serene peace.

CHAPTER IX

Three years of neglect had left their mark upon the Pine Croft bungalow. The stables, the corral, the paddock for the thoroughbred riding horses were in woeful disrepair. The garden was riotous with a tangled mass of weeds and flowers. The water main from the little lake in the hills above, an engineering triumph of Gaspard and the joy of his wife, was broken and the water running in a flood over the lawn.

"What a shame! What a ghastly shame! And the whole place used to be so wonderful! So perfect! It is a cruel shame!" The Colonel's wife was quite petulant over it. "And so unnecessary! Why didn't he pull himself together and play the man?"

"Why? Don't you know? I wonder if you can understand?" The little Colonel's voice was slightly wistful.

"What do you mean?" his wife asked impatiently.

"Oh, dash it all, Augusta! Don't you see? Can't you see? The man's life was broken off short. Why should he—how could he care to carry on?"

His wife glanced curiously at her husband. She felt at times that there was in this loyal, gallant little man something more than the commonplace and quietly controlled gentleman he appeared to be, something she had failed to explore. "He had the place, and——"

"The place!" snorted the Colonel. "Pardon me, my dear. I mean, to one of Gaspard's temperament, you know—well——" The Colonel's voice trailed off into silence.

"But there was the boy," said his wife, covertly watching his face.

"Yes! Yes! Of course, there was the boy," the Colonel

hurried to acquiesce. "Certainly, there was the boy. He ought to have got himself in hand. A shame it was, an inexcusable weakness." His quick laugh puzzled his wife.

"Well, I do wish he would return," continued the Colonel, in a quick change of voice. "The boy needs him, and will need him more and more."

"At least, the boy is not suffering," said his wife sharply.

"Of course, the little chap's quite all right. He has everything he needs. I don't mean he hasn't," replied the Colonel quickly. "Don't imagine anything, Augusta. He's a lucky beggar to tumble into such a home as he has got. But there's his future. He has parts, you know— brilliant parts. And not much chance for development here."

"He is a tremendous responsibility," sighed his wife. "I frankly confess he puzzles me more than a little."

They were on the upper trail, a favourite ride of theirs. On the left hand the wide valley in rich, varied, colourful beauty stretched far across the gleaming river to the purple mountains at the horizon. On the grassy levels could be seen the herds of Saddle-back Holsteins and "bunches" of Percheron horses, mares with their colts at their sides, with here and there a splendid stallion running wild where he had no right to be. The trail climbed up over rough ledges sparsely timbered with pines, then led down into thick brushwood of spruce, cedar and birch, with here and there clumps of sumachs which later would splash the landscape with vivid crimson. Slowly they picked their way in single file along the winding trail, turning down from the high land to the lower road. In the thick of the underbrush Augusta's horse suddenly threw its head into the air, snorted and stood still.

"What's up?" asked the Colonel, drawing level with her.

"Some one coming. I hear horses, and a man's voice," replied his wife, urging her horse forward through the brush into the clearing beyond.

"Good Heavens, Edgar! Come, look!" She sat, pointing with her riding crop at a little cavalcade approaching, a man, a small boy and a woman with a child in her arms.

"My word! It's Gaspard! Gaspard back again!"

On the leading horse the man rode, his face covered with a heavy beard tinged with grey, hollow-eyed, gaunt, his huge frame falling in, and clothed in the ragged, coarse garb of a trapper. It was indeed Gaspard, but how dreadfully changed from the Gaspard of three years ago! Behind him, on an Indian pony, a boy, upright, handsome, with shy yet fearless eyes, his son Peter. And last of all the Indian woman, with a baby in her arms, Onawata, her face as calmly beautiful as ever, yet with lines of suffering deep cut upon it.

"Hello, Gaspard," shouted the Colonel heartily, when he had recovered his breath. "Back again?"

"How do you do, Colonel?" replied the man. "How do you do, Mrs. Pelham?" He bowed low over his horse, removing his slouch hat. "Yes, back again. 'A bad penny,' eh?" His laugh had in it an ugly note. He spoke a few words to the Indian woman, who passed on before with her children, receiving from Augusta as they passed a keen and appraising look.

"Where have you been all this time?" inquired the Colonel.

"Oh," replied Gaspard, with an attempt at nonchalant bravado, "up in the North country, up through the Athabasca, pottering about with the Chippewayans, doing some sketching, hunting a bit, trapping, and the like." He set his hat on the back of his head and looked the Colonel fair in the face, a challenging look, daring him to think and say his worst.

"And—and—how are you feeling now?" The Colonel found it hard to get on, and his wife, sitting her horse straight and stiff behind him, gave him no assistance at all. "You don't look any too well."

"No, I'm not what you would say in the pink. Caught

a bit of a cold, got into my bronchial tubes—exposure, you know, hard living, and that sort of thing. I do feel knocked up a bit, I must confess. I thought perhaps a change to the old place might set me up again." In spite of his attempted bravado his eyes were hungry and wistful.

"Why, it certainly will," said the Colonel heartily, turning to his wife for support. "A few months here in the old place with some one to—that is, with good food and—that sort of thing, you know, will set you up. What do you say, Augusta? He needs to be fed up, that is all."

"Yes, indeed he does," said his wife. "I am sure that Mr. Gaspard will soon recover his strength in these surroundings."

"Well," said the Colonel, "I'm fearfully glad to see you, old man. And you'll come along and put up with us until we get your bungalow in order. Things are a bit run down there and in no shape to receive you. We have plenty of room, and Paul—yes, Paul will be overjoyed to see you. Eh, Augusta?"

"Yes, certainly, Mr. Gaspard. We shall be delighted to have you spend a few days with us." Augusta's tone rather belied her words. "And I am quite sure Paul will be delighted."

"Paul?" replied Gaspard in a low voice, his face contracting as with a sudden pain. "How is the boy?"

"How is he?" shouted the Colonel. "Fit! Splendidly fit! A splendid chap! You will be proud of him. And he will be tremendously glad to see you. He has longed for you."

"Longed for me?" Gaspard repeated the words to himself. "My God!" He sat with his eyes averted from the Colonel's face, looking far across the valley, between the mountains. "I say, Colonel, Mrs. Pelham," he said, with an obvious effort controlling his voice, "could you, would you mind keeping him for a few days, a little while longer, until I get things straightened away?"

"Surely! Surely!" said Augusta heartily. "We shall be more than glad to keep him as long as you can spare him, as long indeed as he cares to stay."

"But come along with us now. You will dine with us and spend the night," urged the Colonel.

"Thank you," said Gaspard, searching his face with his gaunt and wistful gaze. "Thank you all the same, I know you mean it, but I shall camp tonight"—he paused a moment or two as if gathering strength to continue—"at the bungalow. You see," he continued, hurrying over the words, "I am a bit tired, I have a lot of things to do, I am in no shape to appear anywhere, I must get cleaned up. I'm a perfect savage, Mrs. Pelham. I have been living among savages, I have become dehumanised. I must be alone tonight." He raised his hat, bowed with his old grace, and disappeared into the bush.

"God in Heaven!" breathed the Colonel. "What a wreck! Poor devil! Poor devil! What a wreck!"

"Horrible!" echoed his wife. "Ghastly! Horrible! Disgusting!"

The Colonel caught her up quickly. "Disgusting? Well, that's rather hard, isn't it, Augusta? Horrible, yes. Ghastly, too. Poor soul! My heart aches for him."

"You are really most trying, Edgar," burst out his wife. "Have you no eyes? Can you see nothing? Disgusting is the only word."

"Why, my dear!" began the Colonel in astonishment.

"Oh, I have no patience with you," replied his wife. "Can't you see? That—that woman! Those children! And to flaunt that all in our faces here, who knew his wife! Horrible! Disgusting! And yet you asked him to our house! You remember the rumours of three years ago? You were keen then that we should give him the benefit of the doubt. Well, there is doubt no longer." Her laugh was hard and scornful.

"But, my dear Augusta, why imagine the worst? Why not give the man a chance? It may be—there may be some satisfactory explanation."

"Oh, you are quite impossible! Surely one look at that —that—*menage* is enough to sicken anybody."

"What?" said the Colonel in a shocked voice. "Do you think that the woman is not his wife?"

"Oh, Edgar, you are indeed impossible. Let us go home. I am quite ill. Let us go home. Oh, why did he come back? How could he bear to come back to this place, to his old friends, to his son? Why should he curse that boy with his presence, and with all this ghastly shame of his?"

"My God! What will Paul do, Augusta?"

"Paul!" exclaimed his wife. "Good heavens, Edgar! Paul? What can he do?"

"He is only a boy," replied the Colonel.

"A boy? He is twelve years old, nearly thirteen, and in many ways with a man's mind and a man's heart. What will happen, the Lord only knows! The whole thing is terrible beyond words. Edgar, we must think and think quickly about this. And whatever happens one thing is quite certain, that we must keep out of this mess. That is quite clear. No more of Pine Croft for us!"

His wife's lips had assumed that thin line that the Colonel had come to recognise as indicative of the ultimate and final thing in decision.

"But, Augusta, we have got to be decent to the poor devil," said her husband.

"Edgar, in this you must allow me to judge. I am quite decided that there shall be no nonsense about it. There must be no comings and goings with the Pine Croft bungalow. Think of the horrid creature, with that woman and his half-breed children! No! That is all over and done with. Of course, he may come to the house; indeed, he must come once, and we shall have him to dinner. And of course you need not cut him——"

"Cut him?" exclaimed the little Colonel, sitting very straight on his horse. "Cut him? Not if I know myself! That sort of thing isn't done, Augusta, among decent men. We must know the facts at any rate. Besides, he won't trouble any one long. He is about done in. He'll blow out before long."

"The sooner the better! It's about the most decent thing he could do, under the circumstances. Oh, you may look at me! I can't, I simply can't work up any compassion for that man."

For some time they rode on in silence, the Colonel's wife setting a rattling pace and refusing all conversation. As they drew near home, however, she slowed down to a walk.

"Edgar, I want to speak to you quite seriously." Her tone prepared the Colonel for the fixed and inevitable. "We shall say nothing to Paul tonight. I must have— we must have time to think. You may have thought me harsh just now, but the thing is really most perplexing and demands the most careful consideration. You can see that, Edgar?"

"Certainly, my dear. Most obvious, I am sure," replied her husband, fully convinced of impending evil.

"And you will have to make clear to that—to Mr. Gaspard that all interchange of social amenities must of course cease."

"But, my dear, I don't——"

"He will at once see the propriety of the suggestion."

"He would," muttered the Colonel.

"For, after all, he is—he was a gentleman."

"Ah, that is something," said the Colonel bitterly.

"And you will have no difficulty in making clear to him that since he has deliberately chosen to outrage all the decencies of civilised society he cannot expect his friends to ignore the fact."

"Exactly," murmured the Colonel, deeply disturbed at the prospect before him.

"As for Paul——"

"Yes, Paul! You can't think——"

"Please don't catch me up that way, Edgar. As I was saying, Paul must just make his choice. He is quite old enough to understand—make his choice between his father and—and the rest of us."

"You can't mean, Augusta, that the boy——"

"Allow me to finish. You *do* interrupt so."

"Beg pardon, I'm sure."

"I am quite prepared to receive Paul as one of our family. He is a very nice boy and will easily fit in. But there must be no coming and going——"

"But, great Heaven! Augusta, you can't mean that the boy must repudiate his father——"

"Or us. I exactly do." His wife's voice carried the inexorable calm of fate.

"It would kill him to leave his father and——"

"Pooh! Let us not indulge ourselves in heroics."

"But the boy is not to blame. It is not his fault that——"

"No. It is his misfortune. But in that misfortune I do not propose that our family is to be involved. Edgar, do listen to reason. If the boy chooses Pine Croft and his father and—that—that whole *menage,* as I have said, let him choose, but that must end all intercourse with us."

"But why, Augusta? In the name of all that's reasonable and sane, why? A boy like that—I can't see——"

"Oh, Edgar, you can be so tiresome. You can't see? Can't you see that the boy is thirteen—and Peg nearly eleven, and adores him, and——"

The Colonel drew his horse to a standstill. "Peg!" he gasped. "Peggy! Good Lord! Peggy! That infant! Is it that you have been driving at? Well, I'm——" The Colonel's laugh rang out long and loud. His wife, whose horse was now facing his, gazed at him, with flushed face and glistening eyes.

"My dear, you must forgive me," said the Colonel hurriedly. "I apologise most humbly. But, really, you know, the thing is so—so grotesque. Please forgive me. I can't see it otherwise, really, Augusta."

"No, I hardly expected you to see it."

"But those children, Augusta! I do hope you will forgive me."

"Those children? Yes, those children!" His wife's
voice was vibrant with emotion. "In two years the boy
will be fifteen and the girl thirteen. In this country a
girl at thirteen is like a girl at fifteen or seventeen at
home. Look at that Pincher girl, married at sixteen!
Edgar, I know about this—I know!" Her voice broke
suddenly. "No, let me speak," she demanded, recovering
herself with a desperate struggle. "Let those children
grow up together for two, three years—till they are sixteen and fourteen—and the thing will be past our
handling. Edgar, you must give me my way in this. Let
the boy come to us. He will be happy—he likes—us—he
adores you. Or let him go from us. There is no middle
way. Oh, I know—" her voice rose in a cry, "I know,
God knows I know!" She turned her horse quickly and
put him to a gallop, the Colonel following in a maze of
wonder, indignation and confused indecision. The mental processes by which his wife had arrived at her present
attitude of mind were quite hidden from him. Her sudden display of emotion, so unusual with her, paralysed all
consecutive thinking for him. What had come to her?
What unknown, secret spring within her had swamped
that cool, clear head of hers?

He could not know that in one swift backward leap
her mind had cleared the intervening years, and that in
vivid clarity there stood before her a girl of fifteen, in
pigtail and short dresses, wild, impulsive and mad with
a child's passion for a youth, a young subaltern of the
Guards, glorious in his first uniform, who bullied her,
teased her, kissed her and went away, leaving in her soul a
vision of entrancing splendour. Returning two years later,
a handsome, dashing wastrel, already deep in the harvest-
ing of his wild oats, he found it wise to accept a hint from
headquarters and resign his commission. But even so
she was wild to go with him to the world's end. Instead,
her mother, ignoring passionate and tearful protestations,

carried her off on the Grand Tour till the youth had disappeared from his kind, and her world knew him no more. The wound had healed, but the scar remained and in odd moments and in certain weathers still ached. Yes, she knew. And her knowledge steeled her resolve that her child should be spared a like experience, at what cost so ever.

With face pale and set she rode, without further word, straight to her door. As her husband assisted her to alight, she said quietly, "We shall say nothing to Paul tonight."

One glance at her face was enough for him. "No, no, my love. It shall be as you say," was his reply.

"And tomorrow you shall arrange matters with Mr. Gaspard."

The little Colonel looked at her in piteous dismay, but his mind was not working with sufficient celerity to furnish words for an answer.

No peaceful slumber visited the Colonel that night. The prospect of the task laid upon him by his wife, of "arranging" matters with Gaspard, did not invite reposeful emotions. He had sought more exact instructions from his wife as to what proposals should be made to their neighbour and in what terms. He received little aid and less sympathy. It was surely a simple matter, after all. Gaspard had created a social situation for himself which would outrage the whole community. They were still a primitive country in many ways, but they had some regard for the foundations of the social order. The old days when men's passions and desires determined their conduct, with utter disregard of the opinion of decent society, had gone. None knew this better than Gaspard. And all that would be necessary would be to suggest that he must accept the social consequences. "You won't need to rub it in."

"Oh, not in the least. He will probably kick me out of the house," observed the Colonel cheerfully. "And I shall deserve it," he added.

"Oh, nonsense!" replied his wife scornfully. "He is no fool. Of course, I don't mean you men can't meet, and all that. You will do that sort of thing anyway. And you can lay the blame, as you will, doubtless, upon the inexplicable eccentricities of the women. It will only be another burden laid upon our shoulders."

"I wish you would undertake the job," her husband pleaded, "since it seems so simple to you."

"Certainly, I shall if you feel like funking it. Have no doubt about that. And I shall do it thoroughly," said his wife promptly.

"Oh, Lord!" groaned the Colonel, as he swiftly visualised the interview. "The poor devil has hell enough now."

"Thank you, Edgar. It is a dainty compliment. But I would rather give him hell, as you so delicately suggest——"

"Augusta!" protested the Colonel.

"Than allow him to bring hell to my house and family. But that's my last word. I'm going to sleep." So saying she gave her back to her husband, snuggled down under the covers and, with a little sigh of content as with a good day's work well done, settled herself to enjoy the slumber of the just.

"And who will tell Paul?" The Colonel's pitiful appeal broke the long silence.

"Well! I must say, Edgar, you are most annoying, breaking in upon one's sleep that way! Who will tell Paul? I will. Now, go to sleep."

"God help the boy!" muttered the Colonel to his pillow. Then, after a few moments, he said sharply, "I'll do it myself."

"What?" asked his wife sleepily. Then, quite crossly, "Oh, go ahead and do it, whatever it is."

The Colonel's monosyllabic reply was indistinct, but rich in emphasis.

But as is so frequently the case, the Colonel need not have lost his sleep over the prospect of his unpleasant task, for the job fell into other hands than his. For two days he postponed his visit to Pine Croft, keeping Paul close with him under various pretexts. The third afternoon, reading the weather signs in his wife's face, he girded his loins and addressed himself to the business assigned him. With a heart full of compassion for the wretched creature he had last seen humped upon the shaggy Indian pony making his hopeless way through the brushwood in the train of what his wife described as "that horrible *menage*," he rode up to the bungalow in his best military style and whistling a cheerful ditty. So he had ridden upon a Boer entrenchment, at the head of his men, and with a like sensation at the point of junction between stomach and abdomen. He was greeted with a shout from the studio window.

"Hello, Pelham, old boy! Right welcome art thou, most gallant knight! Wilt alight and quaff a posset?" There were not lacking signs that the speaker had been indulging himself in several possets during the afternoon.

"Ah, Gaspard, you are looking very fit, much better than you were when I saw you last."

"My dear fellow, new worlds are born every day. Richard is himself again. Come in and have something. I feel as a snake must feel when he sloughs off the old and emerges in his brand new skin."

And in very truth, the change in the man was nothing other than a transformation. Clean shaven, well groomed, garbed in hunting tweeds and immaculate linen, and with his gun over his arm, he was once more the Gaspard of the old days, handsome, cheery, insouciant, with today a touch of patronising insolence. For Gaspard was now in his studio and among his pictures. He was the artist once more, after three years of exile, and with the divine frenzy stirring in his blood he was lord of his world and of the men and things therein. Certainly no object of compassion, and as certainly no man to approach with a proposal of social ostracism. Small wonder that the little

Colonel fidgeted nervously with his glass and wondered within himself how the deuce he could lead up to the matter in hand.

"Have another drink, Pelham," said Gaspard, helping himself and passing the decanter. "Jove, this stuff has mellowed and ripened these three years. Three years? Three and a half years now. A millennium of hell!" He shuddered visibly as he tossed off his glass. "But it's over, thank God! Over! Jove, it was often a near touch with me. There were days when I dared not trust myself alone with my gun in the woods. Ah-h-h, God!" Again he shuddered. "But it's over. I'm going to paint again —and as I never painted. I have great pictures here," —he struck his breast violently, "angels, devils, waiting release. Devils? Yes, I can paint devils now. God knows I have reason to know them!" He turned swiftly upon the Colonel, pouring himself another glass.

"Pelham, do you believe in the devil?"

The Colonel was frankly startled. "Well, of course, I——"

"Ah-h-h, I see, you know nothing about him. Yours is a sickly abstraction. Well, thank God you don't. But that is all done with. Here I am back where a man can get a bath and sleep in a bed and see the face of a white man. Pelham, I love to look at you, old sport. I'm not saying you're a beauty, but you are white. You're my kind. Have another, eh? No? Hear me, Pelham, it is good to be back home. Thought I'd never have the nerve to return. But—man! Man! to die in a far land with never a kent face to look upon as you go out—I just cudna thole it, as old Jinny would say. By the way, how is old Jinny?"

"Oh, very well. Very useful and fairly happy, I think. You see she has Paul."

"Paul!" His voice lost its harsh, feverish note of bravado. "The boy, you say, is well and happy, eh? Happy? What?" His voice was eager, his look keenly inquiring.

"Yes, Paul is fine and fit and happy. Yes, I'm sure he is happy. Of course, you know, he is awfully keen about you and has wanted to hear from you and all that——"

"Come, let's go about a bit," said Gaspard abruptly, leading the way out of doors. "Can't understand how that main burst. Frost, I fancy. Must put that right. Things are in an awful mess."

"Couldn't help being in a mess very well," said the Colonel stiffly.

"Oh, I didn't mean any criticism, Pelham. I'll have a deuce of a time straightening things out with you. Awfully grateful. Old Tom has told me some and I've seen some too. And then there's Paul." He paused, looking steadfastly at the Colonel.

"Don't say a word about Paul. He has more than repaid any care we have given him. He is one of us, and very dear to us. Indeed, we would be only too glad to keep him with us," said the Colonel, seeing an opening, as he thought. "We—my wife and I——"

"He hasn't been over," said Gaspard. "Does he know I am home?"

"No, he doesn't know. Augusta thought—we thought till you had got things straightened out a bit we would not let him bother you."

"Ah—I see. Very considerate of you both. I appreciate it. It was better, of course. Must do something with that boy. He is what friend Barrie would call a 'lad o' pairts.' But we'll think of that again. A lot of things to do. My affairs are in a frightful mess. Have had a talk with Sleeman. Shrewd chap, Sleeman—devilish shrewd! Must see my banker. Oh, I hardly know where to begin. The old place has run a bit to seed. But I shall soon get it into shape. Some things I want to consult you about, old man—some developments that I have been planning." So he rattled on, giving the Colonel no opportunity of speech, but rushing with feverish speed from one subject to another. They wandered about the stables, noting the decay on every hand, till as they passed beyond the paddock toward the hill Gaspard suddenly sat down upon a fallen tree.

"Let's—sit—a little," he said, his breath coming quick. The Colonel, glancing at him, was shocked and startled at his appearance. His face was a ghastly, pallid yellow, his forehead heavily beaded with perspiration, his hands trembling.

"You're ill, Gaspard. What's wrong? Feel faint? Let me get you something." He set off toward the bungalow.

"No, no—don't go," said Gaspard impatiently. "In—a moment—I shall be—all right. Don't go—a little too much—excitement. Heart rotten—I think. Soon—be—fit." He sat huddled forward on the tree trunk, his hands upon his knees, his eyes staring, fighting for breath.

"Don't worry," he said, striving to smile. "I am often like this. Last—two days—like hell—again. Nerves all—shot to pieces. Sorry you—saw me—like this."

After some minutes' rest, the spasm passed, the colour came back to his face, his breath came more evenly, his hands grew steady. He slid off the tree and lay quietly upon the ground.

"I'm all right now," he said, looking up at the Colonel. "It was this that drove me home from the North Country. One hates to be ill, helpless, to pass out among those heathen, you know. And then there was—Paul." His bravado was all gone. His tone was low and wistful like that of a child wanting its mother. The Colonel was smitten to the heart with pity for him. The thought of the mission which had brought him there was repugnant to him. Come what might, it would not be his hand that would deal him a blow that might well be his death.

Slowly they returned to the bungalow. Gaspard poured himself a stiff glass of spirits. "Ah, that's better," he said, after he had finished the glass. "You see, I can't stand much of a strain, especially emotional strain. Seeing you again, and all that, got to my vitals. I must go softly for a bit."

"You ought to have a doctor see you right away," said the Colonel with decision. "Better let me send you McGillivray, what?"

"No, no. Thanks all the same. I mean to ride down to the Post and see him one of these days. Today and tomorrow I am going to lie up." Then after a pause he added, "The day following I hope to accept Mrs. Pelham's kind invitation to lunch. Then I shall see Paul."

The Colonel's report to his wife was given in a forlorn-hope-now-do-your-worst sort of manner.

"Did you see that Indian woman?" she asked.

"I did not. Would you have had me ask for her?" replied the Colonel, with the air of a man who has dared the ultimate.

"No, dear, you did perfectly right. And it's my opinion that everybody else will follow your example." His wife knew better than to goad a man gone wholly desperate.

The third day at lunch she had her opportunity with Gaspard, but, as the Colonel said, shamelessly crowing over her, nothing was said about the conventions. The Colonel's report of Gaspard's grave heart seizure had driven in her front line. Augusta, however, was merely biding her time. She was still on guard, and waiting a favourable moment to make the counter-attack.

CHAPTER X

The semi-conscious moments of waking to a new day were filled with foreboding for the Colonel. Some horrid evil was impending. It took him some moments to clothe the thing with reality. Once realised, however, its potence was immediate and irresistible. It brought the Colonel sitting bolt upright in bed. With a groan he lay down again, determined to obliterate the spectre in that most completely satisfying of sensuous delights, the luxuriating in forty winks stolen from the morning hours rightfully dedicated to the toils of the new day. In vain. Not one wink, much less forty, could he purloin. Paul was in his mind's eye—Paul now in one pose, now in another: Paul smiling, Paul tensely earnest; Paul astride Joseph and dashing about like a centaur; Paul wide-eyed in wonder, in dismay, in mute, pallid grief, and himself gibbering now in one formula, now in another, the announcement that Paul's father must be ostracised from the polite circles of the Windermere Valley and that Paul must make choice between his father thus ostracised and the "big white house" and its dwellers.

The thing was a ghastly and cruel outrage, imposed upon him by fate inexorable, in the person of his clear-eyed, clear-headed, resolute wife. She was right, doubtless, though the soft-hearted little Colonel could not properly appraise the full ethical value of her arguments. The boy would be horribly hurt, and during those three years the roots of comradeship had struck deep into the lives of both boy and man, perhaps more deeply in man than in boy. They had ridden the valley for long miles together, they had hunted and fished, they had camped, they had boxed together, and in all these the boy had

showed an eager aptitude in acquiring a finish and per-
fection of attainment that had filled his instructor with
affectionate pride. The boy's high spirit, his courage,
his quick, keen perceptive powers, his grace in motion, his
artistic passion for finish in everything he did, had knit
the Colonel's very soul to him. It warmed the little
Colonel's fighting heart, for instance, to have the boy in his
boxing lessons come back again and again with a spirit
that only grew more insatiable with punishment. For the
Colonel was no dilettante instructor in the manly art, and
every lesson ended in a fight that left the boy on the point
of taking the count and the man pumping for wind.

No wonder the Colonel loathed his task. One consideration, and one only, held him to it. Either he must
accomplish it or leave it to his wife, and, loyal soul as he
was, he shuddered to think how very thoroughly and
conscientiously Augusta could do her duty. No, there
was nothing else for it. The task was his, and he would
see it through. He would lure Paul off for a ride and
somewhere in the environment of the open woods offering
distraction he would deliver himself of his message.

But fate, in the shape of a young Holstein bull, took a
hand, and to some purpose.

"There he is again, Uncle Colonel, among the Sleeman
cattle, and you know they roam for ever and ever. Shall
I cut him out?" Paul was pointing an indignant finger
at the young Holstein bull which had broken through the
Pine Croft fence.

"Can't understand how that fence won't hold the brute,"
replied the Colonel. "It is supposed to be bull tight.
Well, he's got a bunch of your cattle with him. We must
quietly edge them along toward the bars. That will be
easier than finding the break. Ride 'em quietly, Paul.
No hurry. Sing to 'em, boy."

Easily the pinto cantered round the herd, gradually
edging the Holsteins toward the bars, the young bull going
quietly enough with them. It was very easily accom-
plished, and after half an hour's cutting out the straying

cattle, bull and all, were within their own "policies," as the Colonel said.

"Hadn't we better run young Braeside into the bull field while we are here?" suggested the Colonel. "I don't like him wandering off all over the place."

"All right, Uncle Colonel, I'll just cut him out," replied Paul, proud of his cowboy attainments.

But the bull had a mind of his own, and with a bellow and flourish of heels was away in a wild race toward the stables and corrals, Paul dashing madly at his heels. The race brought up at the cattle corral, into which Paul steered the surprised and winded animal, where he was made safe for the time being.

"Now, young fellow, you can stay there for a bit," said the boy triumphantly, swinging his pony into a lope in the direction of the bungalow. A hundred yards, and the boy jerked his pony to his haunches and sat rigid, breathless, listening. Out of the bush rode the Colonel.

"You've got him, Paul," he cried, catching sight of the boy.

But, heedless of him, Paul sat his pony as if turned into stone. From the bungalow came a rushing flood of weird harmonies. A look of uncertainty, almost of terror, was on the boy's face.

"What's that—who's that?" he whispered. "It's like—— Is it my Daddy? Daddy! Daddy! Daddy!" His voice rang out in a shrill, quavering cry. He shook the pinto into a gallop, flung himself headlong from the saddle and disappeared within the bungalow.

The Colonel waited, listening, fearful. There was the crashing of an unearthly chord, then silence.

"Well!" ejaculated the Colonel. "They don't need me just at present." He rode up quietly toward the bungalow, dismounted, tied his horse and, pulling out his pipe, threw himself down upon the grass near the door and waited. He finished his second pipeful, then, mounting his horse, he rode quietly homeward.

One part of his task at least was done. There was no

need to break gently to the boy the news of his father's homecoming. But the bite in the announcement still remained. He would have given something to have seen Paul meet his father and to know the reaction upon the boy of Gaspard's *menage,* to employ his wife's designation. Meantime he rode slowly home to his wife, sorely distressed for the boy who had become to him as his own son. The day would doubtless bring its own revelations, and he was philosopher enough to resolve that he would await developments. Later events justified the wisdom of this resolve.

The dinner hour brought Gaspard to the big white house in the proud convoy of his son, to be at first shyly, then warmly welcomed by Peg, an ardent admirer in the old days. During the dinner there was something pathetic in the eager, wistful anxiety of the father to appear quite at his ease and to carry off the situation with his old time aplomb, and equally pathetic in the boy's apologetic pride in his father, whose whole manner somehow did not ring true.

Gaspard was obviously excited and overstrained, eager to please, too eager indeed, and yet insolently defiant, ready to fight. He seemed to be continuously conscious of an air of disapproval, if not contempt, on the part of his hostess. For, do her best, Augusta could not get out of her mind's eye the little cavalcade which had accompanied Gaspard to the bungalow. Hence her disapproving contempt. Why did he bring them back with him? This was the question which, with irritating insistence, kept inserting itself among Gaspard's efforts at brilliant conversation. Not the existence of that doubtful appanage of his, but his stupid effrontery in daring to flaunt the whole thing in the face of his friends and forcing them all to cut him. Augusta had no patience with such stupidity; indeed, she could not conceive how a man of the world could be guilty of any such ridiculous proceeding. It was a crime, not so much against the ethical standards of the valley, but against good form and common sense. In spite of herself, however, she began to be conscious of Gaspard's old time charm. A brilliant conversationalist when he cared, a man of quite unusual intellectual culture, an art critic with a sure touch and true feeling, as the dinner advanced and as the Colonel's generous old port began to warm the courage of his guest, Gaspard's apologetic and wistful air began to evaporate and to give place to one of confident and complaisant ease. He was talking of "art," with a very large capital A, to which he had been led by an appreciative reference to two new Raeburns which had recently arrived from England. He knew the artist's work and his school. Once launched, he was off on a very even keel and with a steady breeze, over somewhat troubled waters, stretching from the pre-Raphaelites to the Cubists. From that to student days in the *Quartier Latin,* thence to his struggles with the hanging committee of the Academy, he roamed with ever increasing confidence and charm. Even the children were fascinated, while the Colonel was jubilantly delighted, for with all her resolution to preserve a coldly courteous attitude toward her visitor, Augusta, herself an enthusiast in art, found herself engaged in a vigorous discussion with the artist over the merits of the modern impressionists, whom she detested, eagerly challenging, agreeing, appealing, with all her old time enthusiasm.

Suddenly Gaspard paused in the full tide of his discussion, caught by the starry eyes of the fascinated Peggy opposite him at table.

"Mrs. Pelham," he exclaimed eagerly, "there's a picture for you. Why not let me do her? I'd love to!"

A grey curtain fell over the animated face of his hostess.

"Portraits are not really my strong suit. But I believe I could do Peg. I know I could. Eh, Peggy?" The little girl flashed a radiant smile at him.

"Come over in the morning with Paul, and I shall have a go at you, eh, what?"

"Peg has her lessons to do in the morning," said her

mother coldly. Her tone drew Gaspard's eyes to her face. Had it not been for his state of exhilaration he would have been warned.

"Well, the early afternoon, then. Though I like the morning light better, and one is fresher in the morning."

"I think we shall not consider a portrait of Peg just now, Mr. Gaspard." Even in his present condition Gaspard got the full effect of the icy chill in her voice. Indeed, the whole table got it. The children gazed at her with wide eyes, questioning. They knew the tone and all its implications. The Colonel hastened to man the breach.

"Very kind of you, Gaspard, I'm sure. We greatly appreciate the offer. Some time a little later—when—a —things have—a—straightened out—a bit, you know. When you get settled down. You understand?"

"Quite. Or, at least, I think I do. I am not really quite sure." Gaspard's tone was a little weary. His voice had gone quite flat. But into his eyes a steely light had come, as he turned them full on the face of his hostess. That lady did not flinch. No one had ever accused her of lack of courage.

"A little thought, a very little thought will show Mr. Gaspard the impropriety of my little girl going to his house for the purpose suggested, or indeed for any purpose whatever." The cold, incisive, deliberate tone cut like razor-edge steel, clean to the bone.

Gaspard shivered as from a knife thrust. His face went white, his lips blue. For two seconds there was silence, then the Colonel took command of the situation. In a voice of quiet, grave dignity he said, "Mr. Gaspard has made us a very kind and very courteous offer, which I most gladly accept." The gallant little Colonel was in his best forlorn-hope form. "The arrangements for sittings will be made later. There are, however, matters which must be spoken of, and tonight. Perhaps the children will retire. It is their bed-time, my dear. Good-night, Peg. Paul, say good-night to your father."

From one to another Peg flitted with a good-night kiss.

With a grave and puzzled air Paul followed her example, reserving his father to the last.

"Good-night, Daddy," he said in a clear, firm voice, putting his arms about his father's neck. His father threw an arm about the boy and drew him close in a quick, strong embrace, and for a moment or two held him there.

"I'm awful, awfully glad you're home, Daddy," said the boy, standing up straight, with a hand on his father's shoulder. "I'm awfully glad. I'm coming home tomorrow after lessons." The boy, standing very straight, let his eyes pass from one to the other of the group about the table, as if challenging each to dispute his announcement.

A warm flush rose to Gaspard's face. "Good-night, boy," he said in a husky, hurried voice. "Not tomorrow, Paul, if Mrs. Pelham will allow you to remain a day or so—" his eyes were turned in wistful appeal to that lady.

"Oh, surely, Mr. Gaspard," she hastened to reply. "We shall be glad to keep Paul as long as he can stay."

"Thank you," said Gaspard humbly. "Good-night, my boy. You will run over tomorrow afternoon, eh?"

"After lessons tomorrow morning, Daddy," said Paul firmly.

"Come, Master Paul." It was old Jinny, who considered it still her nightly duty and privilege to see Master Paul safely tucked away for the night.

"Ah, Jinny! Glad to see you again," said Gaspard, rising and giving her hand a warm shake. "I hear you have been behaving yourself."

"Aw, weel, they that asks a bugler needs yin," said Jinny briskly. "I'm rale glad tae see ye, tho ye're sair peakit like."

"Well, I've had a bit of a cold, but I'll soon be fit again. Well, good-night, Jinny. You have taken good care of the boy, I see."

"An' why wad I no?" said Jinny stoutly. "I held his mither on my knee. Guid-night, sir. Guid-night, mem."

Gaspard stood staring after her in silence.

"A faithful and very worthy old soul," said the Colonel, noting his gaze. "One of the best."

"Yes, a faithful soul—faithful to the dead and faithful to the living." He sank into his chair, covered his face with his hands and sat there huddled and silent.

"Brace up, old chap," said the Colonel, after vigorously clearing his throat. "We understand, and we thoroughly sympathise with your whole position." As he spoke the Colonel faced his wife boldly.

"Thank you, thank you, Pelham," said Gaspard brokenly, grasping the Colonel's hand. "More than I can say I appreciate your sympathy. God knows I need it, though I'm not asking for it." He lifted his head and faced his hostess. "No, I'm not asking for it. I meant to tell you. It is but just to you—to all—that I should. You, Mrs. Pelham, disapprove of me and—of—of my household; not without reason, as far as I am concerned. As to—my—my household, a word or two is necessary. I married this Indian woman——"

"Married!" exclaimed the Colonel. "Good man!"

"Married!" cried Augusta. "But that's different!"

"Ah, you thought—well! I don't wonder you felt like kicking me out. Yes, I married her for two reasons. I knew it was what my dear wife would wish, as an act of justice to the woman and to her child Peter. Also, I wished to do so. She saved me from degradation and despair, and from death by my own hand. Tonight I am saying to you that, while the place in my heart once held by my dear—" he paused a moment with lips quivering—"my dear wife can be filled by no other, yet I can thank God that the woman now in my house is a good, pure-minded, cultured Christian woman."

"My dear Gaspard, my dear Gaspard," said Augusta, rising and coming to him with hand outstretched. "I cannot tell you how vastly thankful and relieved I am. The other thing would have made all communication between our families impossible, as you can see."

"Good heavens! Do you think I——"

"Well, I did think it rather too much, you know. But now I am more relieved than words can express. I shall call—I shall go to see your wife, and shall see that my friends get this thing properly. Of course, you must understand that there will be some difficulty with some of our neighbours."

"I am expecting nothing, dear Augusta. If you can allow the old relations to be re-established as far as Paul and I are concerned and can show a little kindness to my wife I shall be eternally obliged. Poor girl! She too has given up much. The chieftainship of a great and ancient people is hers, but all that she gave up for me—and her children. Now, as to Paul, I was going to ask——"

"My dear chap," interrupted the Colonel in an exuberance of delight, "allow Augusta to tell you what we propose before you speak."

"Well, Gaspard, you know," said Augusta, "believing as I—as we did, we of course felt that the old relations could not very well be re-established. I mean—for Peg's sake—for everybody's sake. There are such things as conventions, and——"

"I know, I know," agreed Gaspard.

"Well, we thought you would allow Paul to make his home—his headquarters—here with us. He could keep on his lessons with Peg. I look after them myself, and he is doing quite famously and is quite a help to Peg, I mean in the way of example and inspiration. Of course, now there is not the same necessity, but if you think——"

"Oh, thank you, dear Mrs. Pelham. I have thought this out during many dark and terrible nights in the North Country, and I resolved that, whatever duty I owed to Onawata, my present wife, I owed a prior duty to my dear wife now gone and to our boy Paul. I am not going to allow Paul's future to be entangled or embarrassed by association with the children of mixed blood. No one can tell how they will turn out. While I am here they will be all right, but no one knows how long I shall be with them. Sometimes I have my fears as to myself.

But as to Paul, I am resolved that he is not to be handicapped nor his future imperilled by the sins and follies of his father. He is a good boy. So if you could allow him to, as you say, make his headquarters with you, it would lift an immense weight off my shoulders and relieve the situation generally more than I can say."

"Splendid! Splendid, old man!" exclaimed the delighted Colonel. "You have put it exactly as it should be put. We shall be more than delighted to have Paul stay with us. Indeed, I should feel it terribly to have to give him up completely. Nothing could be more satisfactory to us, eh, Augusta?"

"I am sure it is the best arrangement all round. Paul has his own future, his own life to work out, and—and—well, I am quite sure you have done the right thing. We shall do our best for Paul. He is indeed like our own son, and a really fine fellow."

"Splendid chap! Wonderful chap! Brilliant chap! Make his mark some day if he lives," exclaimed the Colonel, yielding to his enthusiasm for Paul, and vastly relieved over the solution of a problem that to him had presented the most painful possibilities.

The Colonel's faith in a beneficent, over-ruling Providence was appreciably strengthened by the events of the evening.

CHAPTER XI

The arrangement thus happily consummated had failed to take note of a very important factor necessary to its perfect adjustment, namely Paul himself. It was Paul, with the assistance of Asa, who finally settled the problem of his future.

For some weeks the "big white house" continued to be the headquarters of Paul, where, through a mutual understanding between his father and Mrs. Pelham, he spent the greater part of the day. But no day passed that did not see Paul for some hours at Pine Croft in the company of his father, working up his music according to his father's interpretation of the great masters; reciting his catechism and Bible lessons, for these his father insisted upon more keenly than upon any other; playing with his father's paints and brushes, with now and then a word of instruction as to line or colour, composition or perspective; and struggling with his mathematics, in which Augusta frankly acknowledged that she was rather weak.

His father was eager to supplement in the education of his son the elements which might be lacking in the instruction received at the big white house, which, however excellent of its kind, partook somewhat of the quality and characteristics of that received in an English Dame School. With this idea in mind, the boy was initiated into the mysteries of the elements of engineering, and under his father's instruction began to apply in a series of primitive experiments the principles of the science to road building, bridge construction, water wheels, the laying of water mains, and such like practical undertakings. Many a long and delightful afternoon the boy toiled at construction work, with his father watching while he lay and smoked, occasionally throwing a word of advice or lending a hand.

In these studies and occupations, Peter was his constant companion and worshipful assistant.

Between the Indian woman and Paul hung a veil of reserve which neither seemed able to remove. The woman herself seemed unwilling to take the place of wife and mother in the household. Centuries of tradition wrought in her soul an ineradicable sense of subordination to her lord and master. At the family table Gaspard insisted that she take her place, but inasmuch as the charge of the household duties fell upon her alone she seized every opportunity to serve her lord as the women of her race had served from time immemorial, rather than preside as his equal in the family. This was especially the case at such times as Paul happened to be a member of the family circle, and had it not been for Gaspard's express command she on every occasion would have played the part of servant to her master and the "young chief," as she sometimes shyly named him. Her love for the boy, which was with her second only to that for her lord and master, was a strange mingling of maternal tenderness and of adoration for something high and remote.

As for Paul, he could not have analysed to himself, much less explained to any other, just in what light he considered the Indian woman who occupied such a peculiar place in the household. What that place was Paul, having never been told, was too reserved to enquire. His father had never spoken of it, taking for granted that the boy had understood, and no other had ventured to speak of the matter. For his twelve years the boy had developed an unusual ability to do his own thinking on many subjects, and, moreover, he carried an air of reserve that forbade intrusion into the more intimate things of life.

For one member of the household, however, the sixteen-months babe, Paul developed a swift and absorbing devotion. At his first sight of her the boy utterly lost his heart, and thenceforward was her slave. For half a century of a life teeming with incident and rich in emotion he was never to forget that first vision of little Tannawita—"Singing Water."

It was the afternoon of the eventful day on which he had recovered his father after those three lonely years that he first saw the child. Together his father and he had spent the morning hours, having the house to themselves. After lunch his father, exhausted with the emotions of the meeting, had gone to his room to rest, leaving Paul to meander through a dream world of his own as his fingers wandered softly over the keyboard of the piano. Thus wandering, with face turned toward his father's room, the boy became conscious of the lightest of light fingers touching his arm. Startled, he swung about upon his stool, and there beheld a pair of the bluest of blue eyes, looking fixedly into his through a tangle of curls richly golden. The face made him think at once of the child in a Madonna picture which he remembered his mother to have shown him long ago. The eyes in the picture had the same far away, other-worldly look as the eyes staring so fixedly at him. Hardly daring to breathe, he smiled into the blue eyes, pouring into his smile the utmost magic of his fascination. But the blue eyes gazed, unwinking, unchanging, into his.

"Hello, baby," he said softly, as if fearing to break a spell. "Who are you?"

At once the little hands were lifted up high, while over the face ran rippling waves of light and laughter.

"You are a ripping baby," said the boy, lifting her to his knee. Immediately the little hands went wandering over his face like little gentle living things, poking into mouth and eyes and ears, while from the baby lips came flowing in a gurgling stream the most exquisitely melodious sounds that had ever fallen upon the boy's ears.

"Well, you are a darling," said Paul. "But where in the world do you come from?" He glanced into his father's room and seeing that he was asleep he picked up the baby in his arms and went out into the garden at the back of the house. There upon the grass he lay, playing with the gurgling babe.

The little one had reached the toddling stage, able to move with timid and uncertain steps. In a few minutes the two were deep in a game of hide-and-seek. The baby had curious manners, one with her little hands, carrying them before her face as if pushing something from her. Then, too, she would pause suddenly in mid-career and stand silent, her head forward as if listening intently. Paul had little experience of babies. The only babe he knew was one of a neighbour's, a Mrs. Macdonald, the jolly, kindly matronly wife of a very shrewd and success-ful rancher some five miles down the river. That baby, a sturdy, rosy little rascal about the same age as this, would dash madly after Paul, chasing him round and over ob-stacles with a reckless disregard of consequences. This youngster had its own queer mannerisms which puzzled Paul. Holding by his finger she could race with him freely and with sure foot on the smooth grass, but alone she was filled with timid hesitation. Once he hid behind a tree, calling her. Cautiously she came running, her little hands high in front of her face, halted a moment listening, then in response to a call came dashing toward him and ran full tilt squarely into the tree. The impact hurled her violently upon her back with an abrased nose. Her screams brought the Indian woman from the house, run-ning swiftly.

"She ran into the tree I was hiding behind," explained Paul remorsefully.

The mother caught the child in her arms and, sitting on the grass, soothed her with soft strange sounds till her tears were stayed.

"I am awfully sorry," said the boy. "She must have stumbled head first against the tree."

Clasping the babe tightly to her breast and rocking her gently while she crooned a quaint low song, the mother said nothing in reply.

"I am awfully sorry," again said Paul, puzzled and a little fearful at her silence.

"No," said the mother, when the babe had grown quiet, "she did not see the tree. She does not see—anything. She—is—blind." As she spoke she clutched the babe fiercely to her breast.

"Blind! She can't see anything? She can't see me— now?" The boy was staring, horror-stricken, into the blue eyes once more turned steadily on him. He moved closer to the child. "She can't see!" he said again in a voice shrill with bewilderment, pain, anger.

The mother shook her head, rocking her child in her arms, her face fixed in a look of stony despair.

"Will she never see?" demanded the boy. Again the woman shook her head.

"How did she—who did this to her?" again demanded the boy.

"She was born—this way," said the woman in a toneless voice.

"Born—blind!" The boy kneeled down, looked into the blue eyes, touched with his fingers the uplifted face now turned toward him, then, with a low cry, put his face in the little one's lap. "Oh, God, why did you let her? Why did you let her?" he sobbed again and again. "She's so little—so little."

At the sight of him the woman's stony face broke in tender pity, the silent tears flowed down her cheeks, while the baby's fingers, like little living things, played lightly over the boy's head seeking his face.

In that hour of solemn sacrament the boy in an unspoken covenant dedicated himself to the care and protection of this babe upon whose blue eyes God for some mysterious reason had let this unspeakable horror of darkness fall. Thenceforth no love, no lure could draw away the boy's heart whensoever the babe had need of him. In that hour too the Indian mother of the blind child gave to the boy the deep adoring love of her heart, veil it as she might, second only to that she had given to the man for whose sake she had abandoned home and race and all else that she held dear.

The weeks following the arrangement as to Paul's headquarters were somewhat difficult for the boy. For one thing, Peg was never satisfied that the whole afternoon should be given to Pine Croft, and was continually impressing into her service the Colonel in planning expeditions of one kind and another in which Paul should join. Then, more and more Paul came to see that the days were dragging wearily for his father. Few of the old neighbours visited at Pine Croft, in spite of the vigorous propaganda carried on in the little community by the Colonel and his lady in favour of a generous and liberal judgment of Gaspard and his social misadventures. The only response came from the Macdonalds who, in spite of the stern and rigid ethical standards inherited from their sturdy Nova Scotian forebears, frankly accepted the guarantee of the Colonel and his wife and often dropped in of an evening or on a Sunday afternoon. But it was hard going for them all. The old friends found it difficult to unbend in the old free and easy manners of the old days, without finding themselves involved in reminiscences painful and embarrassing to all concerned. And none of them, with the very best of intentions, could break through the shy, proud reserve of the Indian woman. She had her own life, and between that life and the life of the valley there existed but one vital point of contact, the man whose life she had twice saved and for whom she would gladly any day lay down her life.

Sleeman alone, their nearest neighbour, appeared to be able to establish free and friendly relations with Pine Croft and its mixed household. In and out of the house he was with a familiarity which in the old days Gaspard would have made short work of, but which in these days of ostracism and loneliness he tolerated, even welcomed. Long hours they sat together with, too often, the bottle on the table. Often too a poker game beguiled the hours. Paul hated these afternoons and evenings and hated the

whose visits made them possible. From Sleeman
s very soul turned in revulsion. There was in him the
same quality which Paul discovered in the big milk snakes
which here and there he used to come upon, sliding
without changing shape out of sight into the underbrush.
His son, Asa, affected Paul in a similar manner. Never
with any degree of comfort had he been able to touch
Asa's hand. With Adelina it was different. There was
nothing snaky about her. A biting tongue she had when
it was needed, and a hard-hitting fist when occasion
demanded, but she never showed any snake-like movements. She stood up straight, ready to fight for her
rights and ready to accept a beating when it came her way.
But both father and son Paul kept at long range, and it is
fair to say that the repulsion was mutual. And this repulsion it was that wrought upon Paul's life a potent reaction.

Often in their morning expeditions the children from
the "big white house" and the Sleemans would foregather
and explore some of the many bits of wonderland in the
midst of which they had their homes. Were it not for
Adelina, who was devoted to him, Paul would have
avoided these meetings. And then too, for Asa the dainty,
bright, vivacious little girl from the big white house had
a strong fascination, of which, true to her sex, the child
was pleasantly conscious but the reaction from which in
a continual bullying and teasing she hated. But she
admired Asa for his strength and his ability to do things
men could do with horses and cattle and machinery, and
in her heart she coveted for Paul, whose slave she was,
these gifts and powers. Of course, Paul had compen-
sating qualities which lifted him to a plane far beyond
Asa's poor reach. And she made Asa conscious of this,
to Paul's undoing. For Asa was ever on the watch for
opportunities to humiliate him in the presence of the
others. Yet there was that about Paul that imposed
limits upon Asa's bullying tendencies. Behind the
smaller boy's reserve there lurked a spiritual quality of
mastery that somehow held Asa's coarser nature in check

and made the boy the dominating spirit in the little group. In moments of crisis it was to Paul they instinctively turned.

Notwithstanding this, however, Paul had often sore conflict with himself and was hard put to it to endure the humiliations which Asa put upon him. For in the matter of retaliations Paul was severely handicapped by his religious convictions. The majestic simplicity of the Sermon on the Mount, in such matters as anger and retaliations, hampered him. The impossibility of the *lex talionis* had been instilled into his soul by his mother's doctrine in these matters which, by the way, was quite undiluted by the ingenious refinements of a school of interpretation which sought a place in that sublime ethical code for wrath, hatred, revenge and such like exercises of the human soul. His mother, simple soul, had only one method of interpretation, that of the childlike spirit. Consequently Paul's limitation in the way of the ordinary human reactions to such tyrannies and wrongs as are the lot of the weak at the hands of the strong were serious enough. After much long and painful meditation Paul had achieved a working theory of ethics in regard to rights of freemen under the yoke of a tyrant. He was quite clear about that. He had cunningly extracted from the gallant Colonel his opinion as to legitimate causes for war and he had come to the fixed conviction that, given a worthy cause, war was praiseworthy and right, care being taken to exclude all purely selfish motives. In the early days of Asa's tyrannous conduct, nearly two years ago, Paul made the painful discovery that he was afraid of his enemy. It was then that he had approached the Colonel with the request that he be taught to fight. He hated to feel afraid. It lowered his self-respect immeasurably. More than that, it deprived him of that fine glow of heroic virtue arising from his voluntary endurance without retaliation of many acts of persecution. It was this resolve to overcome the weakening and abasing sense of fear by learning how to fight that spurred him to endure the somewhat strenuous instructions of the little fighting Colonel in the manly art.

It was a glorious September morning and the Colonel was ready for his morning ride. There was a shimmer of heat over the landscape and a promise of thunder in the air. A breathless stillness had fallen upon all things, and over the fields and the distant woods the September haze hung like a thin blue veil.

It had been a successful season on the ranch. The fruit crops had been abundant and through the agency of the newly organised Fruit Growers' Association had been fairly well marketed. The harvest had been quite up to the average, and within a day or two would be safely stacked or under cover.

The Colonel had abundant reason for satisfaction with life, and should have worn a much happier face. His wife, reading his face like an open page, broke forth into protest.

"I don't see why you should go around looking like that," she said impatiently.

"Looking like what?" exclaimed the Colonel, his face becoming at once a perfect picture of radiant cheer.

"Why doesn't somebody do something about it?" she asked petulantly.

"What can any one do? Anyway, what are you talking about, my dear?" inquired her husband, illogically.

"You know quite well. You are worrying yourself to no end."

"Worrying myself? Nonsense! And what about you?"

"The whole thing is about as bad as it could be. The man is doing nothing to his place. Buildings, fences, corrals, everything is going to wreck and ruin. And he hasn't done a thing all this summer."

"My dear, the man is ill. And he is hard up. I happen to know his Bank has turned him down."

"Yes, you have good reason to know," said his wife, with significant emphasis.

"My dear, we won't speak of——"

"Oh, it is all very well, but you can't go on like this. Something ought to be done. That man is about desperate. He may do anything some day. And he shuts himself up in that bungalow from everyone except Paul—and that creature, Sleeman."

"I don't like that fellow. I don't trust him," said the Colonel. "He has the worst sort of influence over poor Gaspard, with his poker and his whiskey."

"My dear, there will be a tragedy there some day, you mark my words."

"Oh, nonsense! But what can I do? Why can't some of you ladies do something for the family?"

"There you are again!" cried his wife, lifting up her hands in despair. "You can't get near her. She is an Indian through and through, proud, reserved. You can't patronise her a——"

"But why should you?"

"Well, you know what I mean," replied his wife impatiently. "Our women went at my solicitation prepared to be quite kind to her. She made them feel—Why, Mrs. Powers said to me, 'She actually patronised us. Made me feel as if she were quite my equal.'"

"And why not?" asked the Colonel simply. "In what is Mrs. Powers the superior of this Indian lady?"

"Oh, I'm not snobbish, Edgar, as you probably know by this time, but——" His wife's voice was coldly indignant.

"My dear, my dear," the Colonel hastened to apologise, "who would suggest that you——"

"Well, I must say it is very difficult. She won't visit. Even her church—she was educated, you know, in a convent—even her church is a kind of barrier. She rides down to the Post all alone when the priest comes. I am in despair. I've tried my best, you've tried your best. The long and the short of it is the man and his place are going to ruin."

The Colonel remained silent. There was nothing to

say. He had tried his best with Gaspard, and so far had failed.

"If he would only brace up," sighed Augusta. "But he seems to have lost his nerve."

"It is the last thing a man loses," replied the Colonel gloomily.

"And there's that boy——"

The Colonel lifted up his hand. "For God's sake, don't speak of the boy. He feels as you do."

"Nonsense! He does not understand the thing at all. He is perfectly happy."

The Colonel groaned. "Great heavens, Augusta, have you not noticed the boy whenever he returns from the ranch? Have you noticed the kind of music he improvises? The boy is worried. He is anxious. He is mystified about that whole outfit. Don't you notice he never speaks of his father now. For the first month his father was his main theme. The thing is really heartbreaking. He spends more and more time there. Some day he will pack up and leave us."

"Well, run away and take your ride. Look up the children and bring them back with you. And *don't worry,*" she added, shaking a minatory figure at him.

"Not I!" shouted the Colonel, and putting his horse full tilt at the bars cleared in fine style and, waving a farewell at his wife, took his way by the river trail out of sight.

After an hour's ride he found himself at the children's rendezvous near the river bend where an open space provided a delightful playground for them. It was the Colonel's practice to steal up Indian fashion and then swooping upon them with war whoop and brandished tomahawk claim, if unobserved till within twenty yards, capture and ransom. With great care he approached within charging distance and was gathering his horse for the final dash when a loud cry arrested him.

"Here you, Asa, stop that! Let him up! Let him up,

I tell you!" It was Adelina, dancing frantically about the boys struggling on the ground, Asa uppermost and pummelling Paul vigorously about the head and shoulders. Her cry unheeded, Adelina dashed in, wreathed her arms around Asa's neck and dragged him backward from his victim.

"You big coward!" panted the girl. "I'll just go and tell pa on you right away." So saying she sprang on her pony and dashed off toward her home, followed by the shouted threats of her brother.

"You called me a liar," said Asa, approaching Paul threateningly.

"No," said Paul, breathing hard, "I did not—but—you did tell a lie."

"Yes, you did!" cried Peg, rushing toward the bigger boy like an enraged mother partridge defending her chicks.

"Oh, you shut up and keep out of this," cried Asa, reaching for her and throwing her heavily to one side.

"You are a big coward!" said Paul, with one rip tearing off his jacket.

His longed for opportunity had come. The law of retaliation for one's own injury was not abrogated for him, but for others, especially for the weak and defenceless, it was a man's duty to fight. His heart glowed with the old Crusader fire. Whether a long series of bitter humiliations added some fuel to the flame he stayed not to consider. His religious inhibitions were withdrawn. A plain duty lay before him. All his fear of the bigger boy vanished. He was ready to be offered a sacrifice.

"Oho! you little liar, you have been wanting a good hiding for some time, and now you're going to get it."

"Peg, keep back!" said Paul, quietly waiting.

The Colonel slipped from the saddle and crept near the clearing, taking his place behind a thick bush.

"By Jove, the boy is going to stand up to him!" he said delightedly. "I hope he'll keep his head and do some foot work now."

The hope was realised. With a rush Asa sought to grapple with his opponent. Paul easily avoided and before Asa could recover had landed one, two, three upon his enemy's unprotected face. The Colonel hugged himself in joy.

"Gad, the boy's showing form," he chuckled in high glee.

Once more Asa rushed, but again Paul eluded him, circling round his man.

"Aw, come on, you coward!" cried Asa. "You dassen't stand up to me."

"Keep away, Paul," cried Peg, dancing excitedly in the offing.

"He'd better!" shouted Asa, rushing after his elusive foe. "But I'll get you all right." But even as he spoke Paul suddenly checked himself and landed heavily with a stiff swing upon Asa's ear as he passed, with telling effect. For a moment or two Asa lay where he had fallen, more astonished than hurt, while Peg shrieked with joy. "Good foot work, Paul!" Not for nothing had she attended the boy's fighting exercises with the Colonel for the last two years.

With greater deliberation the bigger boy set out to secure a clinch with his exasperating opponent.

"Jove, if he can only keep away!" murmured the Colonel. Out and in, back and forward, Asa sought to corner his victim, coming often within touch but just failing to make his catch. The pace was beginning to tell upon Asa, for he was quite unused to this sort of game and his wind was going.

"Now, boy, go in! Go in! Why don't you go——" the Colonel whispered in a frenzy of excitement behind the bush. As if in obedience to the whispered entreaty Paul met a sudden reckless rush of the other with a full straight arm fair upon the chin, lifted him clear off his feet and landed him two yards away on his back, where he lay stretched at full length.

A shriek of delight from Peg greeted the result.

"What a little devil she is!" said the delighted Colonel to himself. "Jove, what a hit, a clean hit! The boy's a wonder! Here, here, look out!" The Colonel's anxiety was well founded. For Paul, dismayed at the unexpected effect of his blow, had approached his enemy with the idea of proffering aid. Slowly Asa recovered himself, raised himself to a sitting position and sat heaving deep sobs, with his head in his hands.

"I'm sorry, Asa," said Paul penitently. "I didn't mean to hit so hard." But there was no response. Asa continued to sob heavily, still with his head in his hands.

"I'm awfully sorry," repeated Paul, drawing nearer. "I didn't mean to——"

His compassion for his fallen foe never found full expression. With a sidelong lurch Asa flung himself at Paul's feet, gripped and hurled him to the ground; then, clambering upon him, held him fast by the throat.

"Now, I've got yeh," he panted, "and I'm going to punch the daylights out o' yeh." And straightway he began pounding his prostrate foe about the head.

Before the Colonel could clear the bush there was a shrill cry, a flutter of legs and arms, and Peg hurled herself upon Asa, wreathed her hands in his bushy hair, and with one fierce swing jerked his head backward and dragged him off his victim.

The Colonel crept back into cover. "By Jove, I'll let 'em fight it out," he muttered. "I do believe they'll handle him."

"I'll get you, you little beast," cried Asa savagely, making for Peg. But before he had taken two steps Paul was on him like a thunderbolt, raining blows on his face and neck till Asa, staggering and bellowing, turned and fairly fled, with Paul hard upon his heels, landing right and left as opportunity offered, till, once more, Asa tripping upon a root tumbled headlong upon the grass and lay groaning.

The fight was over. Asa's bullying days were done.

CHAPTER XII

The aftermath of the fight deprived the gallant Colonel of all his exultation in his pupil's triumph.

"What was it about?" he enquired of Paul as they rode home together. But Paul was silent. His victory brought him no elation. He had done his duty. He had fought in a perfectly good cause and, incidentally, though this he would not acknowledge even to his own secret heart, he had wiped out many a dark and deadly insult endured through many days. But for all that his face was shrouded in deep gloom.

"What started the trouble?" again asked the Colonel.

"Oh! Daddy, Asa is always pickin' on Paul, and today he said—he said—I *will* tell! now—he said Uncle Gaspard was a bad, bad man. And Paul said it was a lie, and——" But at this point Peg caught sight of Paul's face. The look on it was enough to check Peg in mid-career. The boy was ghastly pale, his lips blue and quivering. He pulled his pony to a dead stop.

"He is not a bad man, is he, Uncle Colonel?" His lips could hardly frame the words.

"Certainly not. He is not a bad man. He is a—a good man, but he is having a very bad time."

"He said—he said—" Paul's voice dropped almost to a whisper, "he said—he did—a—an awful bad thing—before—before Peter was born. But he did not—did he, Uncle Colonel?"

The Colonel swore a deep oath, consigning Asa to depths of condemnation unutterable. The boy's honest clear blue eyes the Colonel felt were boring clean down into his very soul. Nothing but the truth seemed possible. He would have given untold wealth to have been able to "lie like a gentleman." But those blue eyes boring into

126

the secret places of his very being disconcerted the little Colonel. He hesitated just a moment, then knew it was too late for anything but straight talking.

"Peg, ride on," he commanded, and Peg, recognising the tone, without question or hesitation obeyed.

Dismounting, the Colonel drew the boy down to a seat beside him and there, face to face and as if man to man, told him the wretched tale, seeing with the boy's pure clean eyes all its sordidness in such light as he had never before conceived it.

An hour passed, and the boy still lay on his face, shuddering and sobbing. The Colonel sat down beside him, striving with word and touch to lay what healing balm he might upon that raw and quivering wound. Gradually the boy's sobbing grew quiet. He rose from the ground, exhausted, white and trembling.

"I think, Uncle Colonel," he said, making a brave attempt to steady his lips, "I'll ride home."

The Colonel searched his white face.

"Paul, you will come home with me tonight," he said firmly, "and tomorrow we shall have another talk."

"Uncle Colonel," said the boy, swallowing, "I think—I want—to—see—Daddy."

The Colonel had handled boys and men in his day, and knew just when kindness was most cruel.

"Paul, you will do what I ask," he said sharply. "To-morrow we shall make our plans."

The sharp tone pulled the boy together.

"Yes, sir," he replied quietly, "but—but—oh, Uncle Colonel, I know now what Mother meant when she—told me—" The boy's voice faltered, he drew a deep breath, stood quietly for a few moments, then continued, "when she told me to tell Daddy—about—the 'seventy times seven.' Poor Daddy!" The brave little voice trailed off into a whisper.

"Come, boy, I want you to be a man, and a brave man. Your father needs you and needs you to be strong and steady."

He could have chosen no better word. The boy's head went up, his shoulders back. He threw the reins over the pony's head, mounted and sat waiting for the Colonel.

"Right-oh!" cried the Colonel. "Let's gallop a bit." They were on the open road and for half a mile the Colonel's broncho raced Joseph off his feet.

"Always thought my bronc was just a shade better than your pinto," said the Colonel, pulling up. But Paul declined the challenge, allowing the pinto to choose his own gait, which for that matter meant a racing pace should the broncho feel so inclined.

Arrived at home they found a household torn with anxiety and a-thrill with the echoes of the battle. Peg must have had a truly blissful hour. But one of the Colonel's quiet words was all that was needed to suppress all curiosity and all undue exuberance of spirit.

Seldom were the conversational powers of the Colonel more brilliantly exercised than through the dinner hour that evening, but with all he could do and with the loyal backing of his wife—for these two never failed to play up to each other's lead—the haggard face of the boy had the effect upon the little company of a ghost at a feast.

"Well, he knows the whole story now," said the Colonel when the children had said good-night. "He wanted to go home tonight."

"And what's this about Asa?" enquired Augusta. "As far as I could gather from Peg's dramatic recital they were all in a general mêlée."

The Colonel's face brightened.

"The boy is a wonder, a perfect wonder, cool as cress and a whirlwind in attack."

"But what happened?" demanded Augusta, whose sporting instincts were deeply intrigued by Peg's version of the encounter between the boys. Nothing loth, the Colonel indulged himself in a graphic description of the battle.

"A clear win, beautifully generalled and superbly handled! Like an old ringer he was. The boy has it in him. And were it not for the horrible fact that that young beast Asa had blurted out the wretched story, doubtless with his own beastly embellishments, we should have all been celebrating tonight. As it is, I know that boy is not sleeping, and I tell you, Augusta, I am quite sick about it. The boy will go to his father. Nothing under heaven will keep him back. He loves to be here, but if it tears his heart up by the roots he will go. The very wrong-doing of his father is a kind of lure. If people are down on his father, all the more the boy will be at his side. And, b'gad, I think the more of him for it. Tomorrow morning the boy leaves us forever."

"Why, in all the world?"

"Point of honour. His father's shame will be his."

"And do you mean to say he will be tied for life to his father's Indian wife and half-breed family?"

"As to the Indian wife, she is as good as the husband, if not a bit better."

"But impossible, Edgar. She will be a burden, a burden impossible. Why should a young boy assume that handicap?"

"Mark me, he'll stick to his father. Try him tomorrow."

The Colonel was proved to be right in his judgment, for, a quarter of an hour after lessons and practice were finished, Paul stood ready at the door of the living room.

"The wagon will come for my box, Aunt Augusta," he said, standing up white and very straight.

"Mother! Mother! He says he's going to leave us! And his father told him to stay. Tell him to stay, Mother." Peg's face was red and indignant.

"And why are you leaving us, Paul? Come here and sit down and let us talk it over."

Paul approached her, but did not sit down.

"Are you not happy here?" Augusta's voice, when she chose, could carry a world of tenderness. Paul's lip trembled. He could not trust his voice, and before Peg he would rather suffer much bodily injury than "cry like a girl." So he wisely remained silent, while Augusta cunningly and carefully marshalled her arguments which she had spent much of the night in preparing. The boy would have often made reply but for his recreant lips which would not keep firm. In the midst of the one-sided argument the Colonel entered the room.

"Daddy! oh, Daddy! he says he's going away!" stormily cried Peg, whose emotions had been deeply wrought upon by her mother's moving argumentation.

"Is he, Peg?" enquired the Colonel gravely.

The Colonel's quiet voice fell upon them like the doom of fate. For the first time since Paul's first announcement to her two hours ago, his departure seemed possible, and, as she looked at her father's serious face, inevitable. With a cry the child flung herself into her mother's arms in a passion of tears.

"Oh, Mother, don't let him go. I don't want him to go."

With a bitter look at her husband, the mother gathered her child into her arms for a brief moment or two, then lightly cried, "Hut! tut! What's all this about? If Paul wants to go home for a while, why shouldn't he go? We'll see him every day. And he will come back again in a few days."

"He will not. He says he will never come back. He says we won't want him to come back. You did," said Peg, glaring at the boy through her tears. "You know you did."

Peg's words released the boy's emotional tension. He glared back at her, indignant that she should thus betray his confidence.

Hoping against hope, but too simply sincere to temporise, the Colonel turned to Paul and, as if talking man to man, said gravely, "You have thought this over carefully, Paul?"

"Yes, sir. I've been thinking all night."

"And you feel you must leave us?"

"Yes, sir."

"But, what nonsense, Paul! Why must you go?" enquired Augusta impatiently.

"I—don't know. Daddy—I think Daddy's awful—awfully lonely," said the boy, dumb misery in his face.

"Why must he go, Daddy?" appealed Peg.

"Why?" The little Colonel rose to his feet, went and stood beside the boy, and put his hand on his shoulder. "You want to know why he must go, Peg?" His voice rang out vibrant and clear. "Then listen to me. He goes because, b'gad, he's a gentleman."

A hot flush surged over the boy's face. He flashed up one swift glance into the Colonel's eyes, a glance of adoring gratitude. Here was a man who could understand a fellow. His head went up and his shoulders back.

"Thank you, sir," he said, and walked steadily out of the house, and for many a day was seen therein no more.

Nor did the Colonel run across him for well nigh a month. For it was well toward the end of September when, riding along the upper trail, he met the boy on his pinto and hailed him jovially.

"Hello, you young rascal! Why have you never been to see your friends? Don't you know you are behaving very badly indeed?" Paul smiled back at him in unfeigned joy.

"Oh, Uncle Colonel, I'm awful glad to see you. I just wanted to see you awfully much."

"Oh, you did, eh? Strange, too. The trail to the white house I believe is still open. And your eyesight appears to be fairly good."

"Oh, Uncle Colonel, I don't know what to do."

The distress in the boy's face sobered the little Colonel.

"Tut, tut, boy! What is so very wrong? I saw your father a couple of days ago and he was looking fairly fit, better indeed than for some time."

"Yes, I know, I know—but, oh, I can't tell you, Uncle Colonel."

"Well, come along, we will ride a bit along the trail. The nuts are coming on fine, eh? Going to be a great crop. We'll have a day at 'em in a couple of weeks. A touch o' frost and they will be fit, eh? I haven't had a good long day in the woods for weeks. We'll take this upper trail. Haven't been to the top this whole summer. The colouring of the valley ought to be worth seeing, eh?" And so the Colonel chatted, giving the boy no chance to make answer. The doings and goings of the family, the ranch operations, plans for the autumn hunting, these all were fully discoursed upon till they reached a bare shoulder overlooking the wide sweeping valley. Already the mountain sides were aflame with the hues of autumn, variegated with the dark green of the massed pines. A truly noble view unfolded itself before them where the valley with its confluents rolled north and south, east and west.

"My! I wish Daddy were here," sighed Paul. "He never paints at all now."

"Ah, not at all?"

"Never. He just sits and sits, looking dreadful, except when I play sometimes, then he tells me how to—to—make it sing, you know, sing like some one singing. That's the way he plays. But sometimes he won't have me play at all. Just hates it. And I don't know what to do."

"What about the fences and stables? Is he not going to get them in shape?"

"He began to, but he gets tired awful quick, and he hasn't got lumber and things. And I heard him tell Sleeman he couldn't get any money. A man in Vancouver wouldn't give him, not a dollar, he said. And he can't buy anything he wants. And Sleeman just laughs and says he's a fool." The boy paused, holding back his wrath, then recovering himself went on quietly. "Of course, Sleeman is a bad man, a very bad man, and I wish he would not come and stay so late. Of course, Daddy is lonesome sometimes, I guess."

"Lonesome? Why doesn't he drop over and see us now and then?"

"He says the neighbours have all forgotten him. But I went with him to the Post and a lot of people remembered him. Jim—Mr. Powers, I mean, and Mr. Macdonald, and Mr. Tom Smith and Jake Smith and Mr. Perrault and old Murphy, Mr. Murphy, I mean, and a lot more men, they all remembered him. But he thinks they have forgotten him. Of course they don't come and sit and talk as they used to when—before—I mean when Mother was here too. Everything is different now, and Daddy just sits and—and—Uncle Colonel, when Sleeman comes—" Paul always forgot his manners in mentioning Sleeman—"when Sleeman comes they just play cards and play and play, and they make such a noise, and Sleeman keeps filling up Daddy's glass. Old Jinny sometimes comes in and just takes the bottle right away. And I wish she would every night, because next day Daddy has always a bad headache. Oh, I wish Sleeman wouldn't come."

The Colonel's face grew grave and stern.

"How often is Sleeman there?" he asked.

"He comes every week two or three times," said Paul. "He's a bad man. When he dies he will go to hell. And it would be better for him to die soon, because he is getting worse every day, wouldn't it, Uncle Colonel?"

"He's no kind of a man to be round your house, at any rate."

"And Onawata hates him. She would like to kill him, I know," said Paul quietly.

"What are you saying, boy?" asked the horrified Colonel.

"Onawata would like to kill him."

"How do you know, Paul?"

"I have watched her eyes. Awful eyes. And it would be better, for he won't repent, of course. And he swears all the time, and you know when he breaks the Third Commandment, what it says in the 'reason annexed.'"

But the Colonel, being deprived of the privilege of instruction in the shorter Catechism in his youth, was quite beyond his depth.

"'Reason annexed?' What on earth are you driving at?"

"You know what the reason annexed to the Third Commandment says, Uncle Colonel, about the breakers of the commandment."

"No," confessed the Colonel. "What does it say?"

"That 'the Lord our God will not suffer them to escape his righteous judgment.' So you see he can't escape, and it would be better if he died very soon."

"Good Lord!" muttered the Colonel, appalled at the relentless theory of the divine administration of the universe. "But what about the Sixth Commandment? Surely that forbids killing."

"No, Uncle Colonel," replied the young theologian, "not always. For it says it 'forbiddeth the taking away of our own life or the life of our neighbour *unjustly*,' and of course it wouldn't be '*unjustly*,' you see."

"Great Heavens, boy! Don't fancy yourself Almighty God. Better leave these things to Him."

"I do, Uncle Colonel," said Paul with great solemnity. "Of course I do."

"Well, keep up your Catechism, but for Heaven's sake get old Fraser, I mean Mr. Fraser—he's your parson, isn't he?—to explain things to you."

"Oh, Daddy explains them to me every Sunday. He makes me say the Catechism over every Sunday, and then I read him my lessons. You know, the lessons Mother used to teach me from the Bible. Except when Sleeman comes—then we sometimes forget."

"One thing, young fellow, don't let your—ah—what do you call her?—the Indian woman, I mean——"

"Onawata."

"Don't let Onawata—a pretty name—get any such bloodthirsty notions in her head, or she may murder the beast some day. Then they'd hang her, b'Jove. Now

I'm coming round to see your father soon. I have been rather busy, but I must come soon. Now let us ride down. Don't fret, and if you want help any time ride over for me."

It was not till the following Sunday that the Colonel was able to fulfil his promise, and it being the Sunday for the Anglican service, which came once in the month, it was late in the afternoon when he rode up to Pine Croft and gave his horse into the care of Indian Louis. Through the open door of the living room came Gaspard's voice, booming loudly.

"That's good for your soul, Sleeman, you ungodly heathen. Say it again, Paul. It will do him good, if he has the brains to take it in. Go on, boy. 'What is the misery of that estate whereinto man fell?'"

High, clear, and with an unmistakable note of triumph in his voice, came Paul's answer.

"'All mankind by their fall lost communion with God, are under his wrath and curse, and so made liable to the miseries in this life, to death itself, and to the pains of hell forever.'"

"That ought to do you good, you old sinner," said Gaspard.

"What about yourself? I guess you're in the same boat," said Sleeman with an oath.

"Oh, no," said Paul.

"Why not?" said Sleeman savagely.

"Because there's 'repentance unto life,' you know," said the boy, with no attempt to conceal his satisfaction.

"And what's that?" asked Sleeman, with a sneer.

"Tell him, Paul. Tell the benighted sinner." Gaspard was hugely enjoying himself. Nothing loth, Paul recited the noble words, 'Repentance unto life is a saving grace, whereby a sinner, out of a true sense of his sin, and apprehension of the mercy of God in Christ, doth, with grief and hatred of his sin, turn from it unto God, with full purpose of and endeavour after new obedience.'

"There, Sleeman, did you ever hear anything more complete?"

Sleeman growled out an oath. "I don't know what the devil you're talkin' about."

Gaspard laughed loud and long. "Of course not, my dear fellow. Have another drink. A man needs brains to understand that little book. That's why the great unwashed gag at our great system of theology. Ha! ha!" Gaspard was immensely tickled at the boy's answer. "Brains, my dear fellow, brains. We furnish the system, we Calvinists, but not the brains."

"All the same, I guess I got as good a chance of missin' hell as you, anyhow."

"No," said Paul again, serenely triumphant.

"And why not?" said Sleeman with another oath.

"Tell him, Paul. This is really great. Tell the blighter, while I have a drink." There was a clink of glasses.

"Because you won't repent," said Paul, announcing a perfectly obvious and cheering fact.

"And what about yourself, you—you——"

"Steady on, Sleeman. No profanity in our theological class. Go on, Paul."

"Oh, you won't repent, you see, and we do. Don't we, Daddy? O' course we do."

The discussion was becoming a little too much for the Colonel, greatly though he enjoyed the apparent perplexity and confusion of the outcast and unregenerate Sleeman, so he made his presence known and entered the room. He was welcomed by Gaspard with acclaim and with urgent invitations to drink, by Paul with vociferous delight, by Sleeman with a reluctant pretence of neighbourly friendliness.

Refusing a drink, the Colonel enquired, "What's doing, Paul? Did I hear you on your native heath, the shorter Catechism? My dear Gaspard, if I am not an expert in Calvinistic theology, the fault is neither that of Paul nor of the shorter Catechism, for the last three years we have had almost daily exercises, Paul and I, in that most terrible and most remarkable book."

"Most remarkable, I grant you," said Gaspard, whose love for theological discussion grew with each successive glass, "but one not easily absorbed by the unschooled Sassenach mind. Sleeman here, for instance, if I repeated to him the immortal and noble phrases which register the answer to the paralysing question, 'What is effectual calling?' would be as hopelessly befogged as if I were reciting a bit of the Koran in its original tongue."

Sleeman squirmed and was silent. When Gaspard was discoursing upon either art or theology he realised his hopeless inadequacy and had the wit to venture no contribution. All the same, it angered him and disturbed him not a little to have his postmortem career outlined for him in the calmly judicial and final manner affected by Paul. His obvious uneasiness under the process gave Gaspard unqualified delight. It was hard enough to be coolly assigned to hell by a youngster who was at no pains to conceal his entire approval of the Divine judgment in the case, but that this disturbing verdict should become the occasion of joyous mirth by his neighbour was, to say the least, irritating. Besides, the homely and relentless logic of some of the "Questions," when rubbed in by the gleeful Gaspard, gave him some serious moments.

But to the Colonel the whole scene was not without its disturbing and depressing elements. Gaspard, for all his cynical hilarity, had every symptom of nerve strain and exhaustion. He was in no condition to run neck and neck with the tough and seasoned Sleeman in a race for the last drop out of the whiskey bottle. It was to the Colonel too a horror that the boy should be forced to endure the sordid environment of a Sunday afternoon spent in so degrading a manner. The thing was obviously hateful to Paul. The boy's whole manner showed high nervous tension, anxiety, even dread. But from the situation there appeared to the Colonel no escape. Paul would stick by his father, and the father was held in the grip of circumstances beyond his power to shake off.

The Colonel sought to turn the conversation away from the profundities of Calvinistic theology into the lighter vein of neighbourly gossip. But Gaspard had imbibed enough from his bottle to be unreasonably fixed in his own opinion of what was seemly in his house on a Sunday afternoon. Moreover, it gave him an unholy joy to see Sleeman flounder among ideas far beyond his comprehension and squirm under the forebodings of an uneasy conscience. As the afternoon passed, Gaspard became less controlled and more provocative and unpleasant in his goading of Sleeman, till the Colonel began to fear a violent rupture between the two. He became conscious also of a consuming anxiety in Paul, mingled with a certain sense of humiliation for his father. Once and again he caught an appealing look in the boy's eyes, till he could bear it no longer.

"Sleeman, it is quite time we were going home, you and I."

Gaspard made loud and indignant protest. "Nonsense, Pelham! You don't come so often. Sit down, man."

"No, we must go. And you are needing rest too, Gaspard. You want sleep."

"Sleep!" shouted Gaspard. "Sleep! Ha! ha! Yes, I need sleep. But shall I sleep? 'To sleep, perhaps to dream! Ah, there's the rub!' The old boy knew what he was talking about. But I know better. Sit down, Sleeman. Don't leave me, Colonel. Sit down—Ah, yes, Paul will play for you, and then perhaps, who knows? I may sleep. Play, Paul! Play, boy! Play! Play!" He was growing terribly excited.

"All right, Daddy. Listen to this. I call it 'Asleep in the Woods.' You'll get it. You'll hear all the things." The boy was excited, too, almost beyond control. He ran to the piano, struck a few crashing chords, then allowed his fingers to rush up and down the keyboard in a perfect fury of sounds, gradually passing into a more moderate tempo and a more melodious theme, till he fell into a movement rich in tone colour, dreamy in motif, varied in phrase, which might well suggest night's many tender moods in the great out-of-doors.

The Colonel waited to observe the effect upon the other two. Upon Gaspard the effect was immediate. Deep in his arm chair he allowed himself to sink, motionless, silent, and buried in thought. The demon of furious unrest was exorcised. As with Saul of old, the evil spirit departed from him, and for the hour at least he passed into peace. With a feeling of immense relief, the Colonel turned his eyes toward Sleeman, and could hardly believe but that his eyes were playing him false. With his face full in the glare of the lamp Sleeman sat, bolt upright, gripping the arms of his chair, held as by a spell, fascinated. Sleeman, material of soul, vulgar in taste, coarse in fibre, there he sat with a look as of another world in his face, as if another soul were gazing through his eyes. Bewildered, rebuked, humbled, the Colonel looked and listened, while the music poured out its melodious song, reminiscent of murmuring pines and running streams under the quiet stars. How long they sat thus, the Colonel could not reckon. It seemed that from some strange and far off country he was recalled as the music passed into the stately solemn chords of Handel's Largo, with which the boy closed his improvisation.

"Good night, Gaspard," he said, as silence followed the music. "Now you will sleep."

"Good night, good night, old friend," replied Gaspard, stretching up a hand from his chair. "Yes, I shall sleep now."

The Colonel touched Sleeman on the arm. "Come along," he said quietly. As if wakened from a sleep, Sleeman rose, stretched himself and with a nod to Gaspard passed out into the falling evening. Together they walked their horses down the avenue of pines in silence.

"Wonderful performance that, Sleeman, eh?" said the Colonel when they had almost reached the road.

"Say, what was that little devil playing there? Ain't he the limit? Say, he's the limit."

"He's a wonderful chap. Made me feel as if I had been in church."

"Say, ain't he the limit? He made me feel like hell!"

The emotions were similar, the phraseology varying as the personality of the speaker.

When the men reached the parting of their ways the Colonel held out his hand. "Good night, Sleeman," he said. "We've had a great afternoon."

"Good night, sir," replied Sleeman, with a new respect in his tone. "Say, ain't he the very devil, eh?"

"That chap Sleeman isn't a half bad sort, after all," the Colonel announced to his wife as he sat smoking his after dinner pipe.

"Sleeman?" ejaculated Augusta. "Beast! That's what he is!"

But the Colonel, recalling the look in Sleeman's eyes, shook his head, a puzzled wonder in his face.

"My dear, my dear, I am not so sure that I am the one to judge. And, thank God, I don't have to."

And his wife, noting the look on his face, ventured no reply. This was one of those rare moments with her when she wondered whether after all the man she had lived with all these years were the simple soul she thought him.

CHAPTER XIII

Over the wide valley the April sun was falling, warmly genial, releasing from the moist earth a thousand fragrances. Under the glorious light the valley lay in dim, neutral colours, except where the masses of pine trees lay dark green and the patches of snow showed white in the hollows between the pines and far up on the grey, rocky sides of the higher mountains. Through the valley the river rolled blue grey, draining from the hills by millions of trickling rivulets the melting snow. As yet the deeper masses of snow and the glaciers lying far up between the loftier peaks had not begun to pour down in spouting waterfalls to swell the great river below. Everywhere were the voices of spring, hymning the age-long miracle of freedom from the long tyranny of winter.

It was a Sunday morning, and from every direction the people were to be seen gathering for service in the little Union Church which the united efforts of the valley people had erected for the use of all who might care to gather for worship. Anglicans, Methodists, Presbyterians, all had equal rights in the church, and each body its day for service. Today was the Presbyterian day, and this day a high day, for it was "Sacrament Sunday." About the door a group of neighbours stood, exchanging the friendly gossip of the valley and subjecting to kindly if pungent criticism each newcomer approaching the church.

"Here's Sawny Cammell in his 'lum' hat," exclaimed Willy Mackie, whom Sandy Campbell would describe as "yon wee Paisley buddie," a little Scot with a sharp tongue but kindly heart.

"'Is plug 'at is for to celebrate the 'oly Communion.

141

(H)it's 'is Sacrament 'at," giggled Sam Hatch, a wizened-up Cockney.

" 'Ere, you cut that (h)out," said his friend, Billy Bickford, a plump, jolly-faced Englishman whose highly coloured and bulbous nose carried its own history. "I don't 'old wi' Sandy in 'is religion, but it's 'isen and let 'im practise it as 'e jolly well wants to, that's me."

" 'Old 'ard, ole top—'oo's a-talkin' agin Sandy's religion or (h)any man's religion. I'm referring to 'is 'at, wich I might saigh I wish I 'ad the like of it. I (h)ain't no 'eathen, I (h)ain't."

"All right, Sammy, all right. I'm not persoomin' to suggest (h)any such thing, but I'm sensitive about Sandy's religion and (h)anything belongin' to it. Wot about 'is minister? Wot about 'im, eh? That's wot I (h)asks, wot about 'im?" Billy's eyes were ablaze.

Behind Billy's sensitiveness lay a story known to every one in the valley. A story of a long, long fight against odds between Billy and his bottle, in which the minister played a somewhat effective part. And another story, a sad one to Billy and to Billy's mild little wife, a story of a diphtheria epidemic in the valley, of three children down with it one after another, with the mother in bed with a fourth newly born, of long watches shared by two desperate men, of which the minister was one and Billy the other, and of two graves in the churchyard near by. From the day those graves were closed Billy was "sensitive" upon any matter touching Donald Fraser however remotely.

" 'Is minister? 'Is minister?" cried Hatch, quite familiar with Billy's story. "Look 'ee 'ere, Billy, don't you go for to make me saigh wot I didn't saigh. Wot's 'is minister got to do with 'is 'at? Tell me that. An' don't you——" The little man's indignation made him incoherent.

" ' 'Is Sacrament 'at,' says you," replied Bickford, attempting a dignified judicial calm. " 'Is Sacrament 'at 'as to do wi' 'is Sacrament, and 'is Sacrament wi' 'is Church, and 'is Church wi' 'is minister."

"Lor'-a-mercy, 'ear 'im! Why stop at 'is minister. Why not go on to 'is minister's yeller dog?" fumed Hatch, highly incensed at being placed in an attitude of criticism toward Sandy's minister. " 'Oo's a-talkin' about 'is minister, I (h)ask?"

"I (h)accept y're apology, Sammy," replied Billy, with gracious condescension, "and we will consider the subject closed. Good morning, Mr. Campbell. It is a rare fine Sunday morning for the Sacrament." He went forward with hand outstretched in welcome, leaving his friend Hatch choking with unexpressed indignation.

"Good morning, Mr. Bickford," replied Sandy, an undersized Highlander dressed in his "blacks" and, as has been indicated, with a "plug" hat on his head, whose ancient style and well-worn nap proclaimed its long and honourable service. "It is indeed a glorious morning for the Sacrament, to such as are worthy to enjoy it." The Highlander's eyes were deep blue in colour and set deep in his head, under shaggy eyebrows. They were the eyes of a mystic, far looking, tender, yet with fire lurking in their depths. "Aye, for such as are worthy to partake," he echoed with a sigh, as he passed to a place beside his friend, big John Carr, a handsome, slow-moving South Country Scot, where he stood lost in introspection.

"I guess Sandy has the pip this morning," said a tall young fellow, Tom Powers, with a clean-cut, clean-shaven brown face and humorous brown eyes.

"I doot he'll be better aifter the service. He has an unco' low opeenion o' himsel'," said John Carr in an aside to Powers. "But he's nae sae bad, is Sandy."

"Oh, Sandy's all right. He's got his Sunday clothes on, and they depress him a bit. And no wonder. They do every fellow. Hello, here's the Colonel and his democrat. Got a new coat of paint, eh? Sure sign of spring."

Down the road the Colonel could be seen driving a spanking team of bay roadsters in a light two-seated democrat, shoulders back, elbows squared, whip-aflourish, altogether making a very handsome appearance. At a smart pace he swung his bays into the churchyard and drew up at the alighting platform, throwing his foam-flecked steeds upon their haunches.

"Look at that now!" exclaimed Tom Powers, sotto voce. "What's the matter with the British Army?"

As he spoke the young fellow stepped forward and gave his hand to the Colonel's wife to assist her from the platform, then lifted Peg down from the wagon, swinging her clear over the platform to the grass.

"Good morning, Mrs. Pelham. Mighty fine outfit, Colonel. You do the valley proud."

"Ah, how are you, Powers? What? Not too bad a match, eh?" He tchicked to the bays, holding them on a firm rein. Well they knew what was expected of them. On their hind legs they stood poised a moment or two, then in a series of dainty prancing steps they were off toward the shed. It was a part of the Colonel's regular Sunday morning display.

Following close upon the Pelhams came Gaspard and Paul. A murmur ran round the waiting group. Not for nearly four years had Gaspard been seen at church, not since the tragedy of his wife's death which had shocked the whole valley. His presence today was the result of the efforts of his minister, Donald Fraser, formerly a great friend of his late wife, backed up by the persuasions of Paul who had refused for the past six months to go to church without his father. This was Paul's birthday and as a treat for the boy he had finally consented to come. But there was more than his regard for his minister and his love for his son in his consenting to come. The past year had been one of stern discipline to Gaspard. Ill health, loneliness, the stress of poverty, the sense of ill desert had overwhelmed him in a flood of misery. Then came Donald Fraser back into his life, from which he had been vehemently driven out, refusing to abandon him. Every third week as the day of the

Presbyterian service came round the buckboard and the yellow buckskin broncho drove up to the Pine Croft stables.

"You need not glower at me, Gaspard," he had said the day of his first appearance. "I am coming to visit you, for your sake because you need me and for your boy's sake who wants me. No! I'll not put my horse in. My duty does not make it necessary that I should force myself upon your hospitality."

But Gaspard had only sworn at him and replied, "Don't be a bally ass, Fraser. I'm not taking much stock in your religion, but I don't forget my—my family's friends. Louis, put the minister's horse up."

From that day Fraser felt himself entitled to turn into the Pine Croft drive when in the neighbourhood. And many an hour, happy and otherwise, did he spend with Gaspard, fighting out the metaphysics of the Calvinistic system in which he was a master, and with Paul over his music, for the minister was music mad. Nor did he fail to "deal faithfully" with Gaspard, to the good of the rancher's soul. One result of Fraser's visitations and "faithful dealing" was the loosening of Sleeman's grip upon Gaspard's life. It took but a very few visits to lay bare to the minister's eye the tragedy of degeneration in Gaspard to whom in other and happier days Sleeman had been altogether detestable.

"Go and see the man. He is lonely and sick and devil ridden," he commanded the men of the valley, and they obeyed him. Under the humanising influence of genial friendliness Gaspard gradually came nearer to being himself again.

So it came that here he was once more at church, to the great satisfaction of the whole body of his acquaintances of other days, but chiefly of his son, to whom this Sunday morning, this radiant birthday morning of his, was like a gift sent straight from the blue heaven above. On every side Gaspard was welcomed with more effusion than was common among the men of the valley. And the reason for this was that Donald Fraser had been setting before them in no uncertain manner their hypocrisy and Pharisaic self-righteousness in shunning a man who was a sinner differing from them only in this, that his sin happened to be known.

Paul waited only to witness his father's welcome, then slipped in to his old place at the piano, which served as an organ, to which Billy Bickford conducted him in semi-official state, for Billy was a church warden for the Anglican part of the congregation. In a moment or two, through the open windows there streamed out a rippling flow of joyous music. As the gay song of spring came rippling through the windows Sandy Campbell started forward with a word of indignant protest.

"Haud ye fast a bit, man," said John Carr, laying a big detaining hand upon the Highlander's arm. "The laddie is just tuning a wee."

"Tuning? And iss that what you will be calling yon? I tell ye, John, I love the laddie and his music, but iss yon thing a suitable music for the house o' God on the Lord's day?"

"Haud on a wee, Sandy man!" adjured his friend. "Gie the laddie time tae draw his breath."

"What's that reel, Sandy?" inquired Tom Powers, cocking a critical ear toward the window. "Sounds a little like 'Tullochgorum' to me. But I ain't Scotch, though my mother was."

Sandy squirmed in the clutch of John Carr's big hand, under the gibe.

"No, that must be Lord Macdonald's—di-del-di, di-del-um," hummed Powers, tapping an ungodly foot in time with the music.

"John Carr, take your hand from my arm. This iss no less than desecration, high desecration, I am telling you. The laddie has gone mad," cried Sandy, greatly distressed and struggling to free himself from Carr's calm grip.

"Listen to what he's playin' the noo," said Carr quietly.

As he spoke the rippling dance of the spring music had given place to the simple strains of an old-fashioned "bairns' hymn." As the three men stood listening, each became aware of the subtle changes in the faces of the others, but they knew not how upon their own faces were registered emotions which they would have hid from all the world.

The lines of stern disapproval in Sandy's face softened into those of tender reminiscence. John Carr's placid face became gravely sad, as his eyes wandered to a far corner of the churchyard. While Tom Powers turned abruptly toward the church door, whither Sandy had led the way. Over and over again the bairns' hymn stole like a far-away echo over the congregation in major and minor keys, then glided into the more stately and solemn cadences of the great Psalms and hymns of the Church Universal.

One by one the people about the door passed quietly into their places in the beautiful little church, and there sat listening till the minister appeared. It was one of the great hours in Paul's life, restored to him again after months of absence from church. As the minister bowed his head in silent prayer the piano began, in tones tremulously sweet, the minor strains of that most poignantly penitential air of all Scottish psalmody, Old Coleshill, a fitting prelude to the ritual, tender, solemn, moving, of the ancient Scottish Communion Service.

The sermon was less profoundly theological than usual. The theme, as ever on a Sacrament Sunday, was one of the great doctrines of the Cross, "Forgiveness, Its Ground and Its Fruits." And while the preacher revelled in the unfolding of the mysteries the congregation, according to their mental and spiritual predilections and training, followed with keen appreciation or with patient endurance till the close.

To the superficial and non-understanding observer the Scot "enjoys" his religion sadly. His doctrinal furnishing is too profoundly logical and his moral sense too acutely developed to permit him any illusions as to his standing before his own conscience and before the bar of Eternal Righteousness, and while in other departments of life his native consciousness of merit in comparison with that of inferior races renders him impervious to the criticism of other people—for how can they be expected to know?—and alleviates to a large extent even his own self-condemnation at times, when it comes to "matters of the soul" he passes into a region where he stands alone with his God in an ecstasy of self-abasement which may in moments of supreme exaltation be merged into an experience of solemn and holy joy. But these moments are never spoken of. They become part of his religious experience, never to be revealed.

By the gleam in Sandy Campbell's deep blue eyes the expert might have been able to gather that Sandy was on the way to ecstasy. Gaspard, though not of Sandy's mystic type, had in him enough of his Highland blood strain to respond to the Celtic fervour of Donald Fraser proclaiming the mystery of the vicarious passion of the Cross. Today the usual commercialised aspect of the great doctrine was overwhelmed in the appeal of the Divine compassion to wayward and wandering children. The minister was more human, less academic, in his treatment of his great theme than was his wont. Paul, seated at the piano, was apparently quite undisturbed by the profundities of the minister's discourse. To him the refinements and elaborations of theological propositions were so much waste of words. Sin, judgment, repentance, forgiveness, were simple and easily understood ideas. They had entered into his daily experience in his earlier days with his mother. With God it was just the same thing. Why fuss about what was so abundantly plain that any child might take it in? Today he was watching his father's face and Sandy Campbell's. He was interested in their interest and enjoying their enjoyment. His face reflected their moods and emotions. The minister's eye was caught and held by the boy's face, and all unconsciously his sermon took tone and colour from what he found there.

The communion hymn was followed by an abbreviated —for time pressed—but none the less soul-searching address, known in old-time Presbyterian parlance as the "Fencing of the Table." This part of the communion "Exercises," however necessary in communities only nominally religious and in times when "coming forward" had come to be regarded as a purely formal duty associated with the attaining of "years of discretion" rather than with any particular religious experience, the minister during his years in the valley had come to touch somewhat lightly. Among the people of the valley there was little need of a "fence" to warn back the rashly self-complacent from "unworthily communing." Yet custom dies hard in matters religious, and in consequence the "Fencing of the Table" could not be neglected. Encouraged by the invitation to the holy ordinance given with a warmth and breadth of appeal to "all who desired to remember with grateful and penitent heart the Lord Who had given His life for them," Paul, without much previous thought and moved chiefly by the desire quite unusual at such a moment to share in the solemn service with his father, who apparently had suddenly resolved to renew his relation to his faith and to his Church to-day, had slipped from the piano seat to his father's side. During the "fencing" process, Paul's mind, borne afar upon the spiritual tides released by the whole service and its environment and quite oblivious to the argument and appeal in the words of the address, was suddenly and violently arrested by a phrase, "You must forgive him who has wronged you, else you dare not partake." As the idea was elaborated and enforced with all the fervent passion of the minister's Highland soul the boy's whole mental horizon became blocked with one terrible and forbidding object, the face of Asa Sleeman. The sin of the unforgiving soul daring to enter into communion with the forgiving Lord was pressed with relentless logic upon the boy's conscience. An overwhelming horror fell upon him. Forgive him who had uttered the foul lie about his father? The thing was simply a moral impossibility. The whole moral order of his Universe would in that case come tumbling in ruins about him. The thing called for judgment, not forgiveness—judgment and condign punishment. Wrong things and wrong people must be punished, else what was hell for? Yet, "forgive him who has wronged you," the minister was saying, "else you cannot be forgiven." Clearly there was no hope for him. His whole theory of forgiveness and restoration was rudely shattered. Asa and his father might possibly escape hell after all. It was a disturbing thought. At any rate, the communion was not for him. He glanced hastily at his father.

"I am going out a bit," he whispered.

"Are you ill?" inquired his father, startled at the pallor in his face.

"No, I'm all right," he replied, and rising quietly he passed out and through the open door of the church.

The "Fencing of the Table" was concluded in as thorough a manner as the conscience of the minister demanded. The solemn moment when the elders were to go forward for "the administration of the elements" had arrived. From his place near the front of the church John Carr had risen, expecting his fellow Elder, Sandy Campbell, to join him in his impressive march to the "Table." Sandy, however, was nowhere to be seen. The situation was extremely awkward.

"Is Mr. Campbell not present?" inquired the minister, scanning the congregation.

"'E's retired from the church, sir," replied Churchwarden Bickford, respectfully rising from his seat, "but if I might (h)assist—" he added with a hesitating glance at John Carr.

"Thank you, Mr. Bickford, if you would be so kind—" began Mr. Fraser. "Ah! here is Mr. Campbell," he added, greatly relieved. A church warden might possess in full measure the qualifications necessary for his exalted office, but as a substitute for an Elder in the administering of the Sacrament he left something to be desired.

Quietly and with impressive deliberation Sandy made his way to the "Table" while under cover of the ceremonial of "preparing the elements" Paul slipped quietly into his place beside his father.

"And whaur did ye flit tae, Sandy?" inquired John Carr as they two were "daunderin'" homewards after the service. "Man, it was a terrible embarrassment tae hae yon Bickford buddie offer to officiate."

"It wass the lad. He wass driven out from the 'Table,' but by what spirit I wass unable to judge till I had inquired." For some distance Sandy walked on in silence and his friend knew him well enough to await his word. "He was under deep conviction and sore vexed, but he was brought out into a large place." Still John Carr walked on in silence. These matters were to be handled with delicacy and reserve.

"Yess! the word wass given me," said Sandy softly. "Oh, yess! even to me. 'Out of the mouth of babes and sucklings.'"

"He is a wise laddie in spite o' quirks," ventured his friend.

"'Quirks'?" inquired Sandy with some severity. "'Quirks' did you say? And what might you be calling 'quirks'? The lad is a rare lad with a gift of discernment beyond his years. I went out in my pride of heart to minister counsel to him. I found that it was for myself that he had the word of the Lord. And a searching word it wass. Oh, yess! yess!"

"Hoots! Sandy, he wad na presume to instruct an Elder." John Carr was plainly shocked at the possibility.

"Instruct? What are you saying? The lad had no thought of me whateffer. I found him away back beyond the church, wailing like a bairn that had lost its mother, because, mark you! he was unfit to join with the people of God in remembering the Lord. John Carr, I will confess to you as I did to the Lord Himself that I was stricken to the heart for my pride and self-sufficiency as I heard him crying after his God. Truly, the Lord was gracious to me, a hard-hearted sinner, in that moment. For on my knees I made confession of my sin before God —till the lad himself gave me the word."

"And what word was that, Sandy?" ventured John Carr, for Sandy had fallen into silence.

"It wass the Lord's word to my soul, John, and I will not be repeating it. But it brought the light whateffer."

"The laddie came forward I observed."

"Oh, yess, yess, he came forward. It was given to me to remove some slight misconceptions from the lad's mind as to the Divine economy in the matter of mercy and judgment, and he came forward. It was irregular, I grant you, but who was I, John Carr, to forbid him the 'Table' of the Lord?" Halting in his walk, Sandy flung the challenge at his friend's head and waited for reply.

"Tut! tut! Sandy, I'm no saying ye did onything but right tae bring in the lad," protested Carr.

"Indeed and indeed, he was the one who brought me in. 'A little child shall lead them.' John, John, it iss myself that iss in sore need of leading. And that have I learned this day."

And no further enlightenment on the matter would Sandy offer that day.

But it would have helped John Carr to a better understanding of what had really transpired at the back of the church that day had he overheard Paul's words to his father as they rode home from the church.

"Say, Daddy, I never knew Sandy Campbell—Mr. Campbell, I mean, was like that."

"Like what, Paul?"

"Well, he's funny, you know, but he is awful, awfully nice. He understands a fellow so quick—and—you know, Daddy, he made me think of—I mean he talked to me——

Daddy, Tom Powers makes fun of him but I think he's just splendid."

"How do you mean?" asked his father.

The boy was silent for some moments and then said shyly, "I don't know exactly. Oh, he is just splendid, Daddy!" he exclaimed with a rush of enthusiasm. "He talked to me just like mother used to."

"Did he, boy?" said his father, with a sudden choke in his voice. "Then he must indeed be splendid."

CHAPTER XIV

The Reverend Donald Fraser was pushing his buckskin broncho faster than he really liked, but he was late for his next appointment and he had to run in to Pine Croft for a hurried meal. Gaspard had insisted upon this, and the unique experiences of the morning strongly inclined him to this course.

The morning had furnished one of the rare oases which here and there dotted the otherwise somewhat dreary landscape of his ministerial experience in the Windermere Valley.

The recall of Gaspard to his place in the church had undoubtedly been an event of quite impressive importance with the minister, just as the moral and physical collapse of the rancher had dealt a heavy blow to the cause for which the minister stood in the community. The unexpected and voluntary forward step in the religious life taken by Paul too had furnished an additional exhilaration in the experiences of the morning. Paul had been to him somewhat of an enigma. He had never met with just such another in all his forty years of varied service in the slums of Glasgow and on the mission fields of the West. But he had been none the less delighted, indeed thrilled, by the act of the boy in making his first communion in this rather irregular and startling manner. The boy was all right. The training of a wise and saintly mother had furnished the mould for his soul stuff that would determine his character and destiny. He wanted a word with both father and son before the first impressions of the day had been dissipated. He believed in striking while the iron was hot.

So urging his buckskin to unusual speed he turned

into the Pine Croft drive and in his old buckboard rattled up toward the bungalow.

As he turned toward the stables the figure of a man, wildly dishevelled, hurled itself down the front steps and rushed toward a horse tied at the garden gate. It was Sleeman, white of face, wild of eye, mad with fear, and rushing as if hunted by ten thousand devils.

"What's wrong? What's up, Mr. Sleeman?" cried the minister, pulling his horse to a standstill.

As he spoke there came from the bungalow a succession of piercing cries, weird, wild, unlike anything he had ever heard, then the sound of a shot, then a long, loud wailing.

"God help us! What is that?" cried Mr. Fraser, making for the door. "Wait, you may be needed." But Sleeman, tearing at the reins, had got them free and, flinging himself across his horse, swung off down the drive. Before he could get under way forth from the door came Paul, a smoking gun in his hand, cleared the steps at a single bound, and, eluding the grasp of the minister, rushed through the gate and pulled his gun upon the flying horseman. The shot went wide, a second and a third failed of the mark. The fourth shot found the foreleg of the horse. The animal stumbled, recovered itself, then finally plunged headlong to earth, flinging its rider heavily to the ground. With a glad yell the boy ran swiftly forward, his gun held steadily in position, waiting for the man to rise. But before he could get his "bead" the minister, shouting "Paul! Paul! don't shoot! don't shoot, boy!" had covered the intervening space and reached the boy's side, just as the fleeing man struggled on the road side to his feet and running low made for the bushes.

As the minister touched the boy's arm the flame leaped from the gun muzzle, the flying figure stumbled, fell, rose and disappeared in the underbrush.

"Paul! Paul! what are you doing? Stop! Stop! Listen to me, Paul." The minister's arms were thrown around the boy. But like one possessed and with a man's strength the sinewy muscles writhed free from the encircling arms.

Breathless, bewildered, the boy stood a moment, summoning his wits and his strength, when from the doorway a voice came gasping, "Paul, boy! I want you."

"Daddy!" cried the boy, and flinging his gun down he ran toward his father.

"Daddy! oh, Daddy, dear! are you hurt?" He caught his father in his arms and held him fast.

As the minister reached the door Gaspard, clinging to his son, sagged slowly down to the floor and lay white and gasping for breath. A hasty examination showed a wound in the side, from which blood was slowly trickling.

"Paul, take my horse and go for Colonel Pelham, and have him send for the doctor."

Without a word Paul ran swiftly to the back of the house, found his pinto waiting, mounted and was off at top speed down the drive.

Within an hour, by a rare chance, the doctor was found and in attendance.

"How did this thing happen?" he inquired.

"Tell me, Doctor, is this the end?" said Gaspard, speaking as calmly as if asking about the weather. "Don't lie to me, Doctor. You needn't, you know. I know your professional tricks. 'Keep the patient quiet,' and all that stuff."

"Gaspard, you have a chance, if you want to take it," said the doctor, patting his patient on the arm.

"Doctor, I want to live—to try once more to make good —for the boy's sake. But, Doctor, I have a queer feeling here." He laid his hand on his heart. "I think I am done for, eh? What about it, old friend? The truth, Doctor. Only the truth will do. If I am going out I have some things to do while I can. Doctor, I am no coward." His eyes were quietly searching the doctor's face. There was in them deep concern but no fear. In the silence could be heard the ticking of the doctor's big watch. The doctor's face began to twitch.

"Thank you, Doctor, that will do. Now how long have I?"

"Three hours, perhaps six, Gaspard old man. You have a right to the truth," said the doctor, taking himself in hand with a firm grip.

"Again, thank you. I knew you wouldn't fail me. Now, a little business. Doctor, you watch my time." The doctor nodded.

"Where's Pelham? Ah, Colonel, I am going to ask you to take charge. It is an infernal nuisance, but——"

"A pleasure! Eh—confound it! I mean, I shall willingly do all I can," replied the Colonel hurriedly.

"First of all, Gaspard, before anything else, tell me how this happened. This is necessary," said the doctor.

"Surely, surely, take it down—Paul and I riding home from church found my wife struggling in the grip of that devil Sleeman—she defending herself with her hunting knife—seeing them I sprang for gun, hanging on the wall—the beast made a break for the door—my wife threw herself on me, catching my gun hand—in the struggle the gun went off—the gun fell on the floor—Paul grabbed it and very nearly did what I would have done. He's a little better shot than I—glad he didn't get him. That's all. Paul saw everything. Paul! Listen! There must be no more of this—remember!"

Paul started from the bedside where he had been kneeling and stood tense and rigid.

"What, Daddy?" he said. "You know, Daddy, I must kill him. He deserves to be killed. It is right, Daddy." The boy spoke quietly with the steady voice of a man set upon a simple and irrevocable duty. His father's eyes rested with loving pride on his boy's face for a moment or two.

"Good boy!" he said, laying his hand on the boy's shoulder. "Good boy! And you will be a good man— a better man than your father."

"Daddy! Don't, Daddy!" The boy's voice broke in a cry of pain. The Colonel's head went down on the bed.

"Steady, every one!" said the doctor in a strong, clear voice. "Don't waste his strength." It was the word needed for the moment.

"Paul, my boy," pleaded Gaspard. The boy stood, it seemed for minutes, his hands writhing, his burning eyes upon his father's face, his lips closed in a thin white line. His father put out his hand to him. "You promise, Paul?"

"A-a-ah!" A long-drawn sigh that seemed to carry in it the outgoing of his very soul came from Paul's white lips. "Yes, Daddy. Oh! yes! I promise."

"Good boy! good boy!" whispered his father, drawing the boy down to him. "I knew! I knew!"

For a long time no one spoke, for Gaspard lay as if exhausted, with eyes closed, voiceless and hardly breathing. After he had rested, Gaspard, always husbanding his strength under the doctor's care, went over his affairs with the Colonel, turning over everything to his charge.

"There should be something left from the wreckage, Pelham. Not enough, perhaps, but it will all go to Paul. Paul will take care of the others, won't you, boy?"

"Yes, Daddy, I will," replied the boy, accepting without question a trust that was to determine for him the course of his life at more than one moment of crisis.

When he had finished with the arranging of his affairs Gaspard called his Indian wife and her children to him. At once the others moved into another room. No one witnessed that farewell, not even Paul. For an hour the woman sat beside the man who was to her life as the sun to the flowers. Almost without speech, without tears or moan or lament, she sat, now with her head pressed down upon his hand, again with his hand pressed hard against her breast, watchful not to weary him or exhaust his failing strength with her grief. Beside him on the bed sat the little blind child, her inquiring little fingers wandering over his face as his voice changed with his pain.

Beside his mother sat Peter, silent, stoical, after the manner of his mother's race. Before he sent them away for the last time Gaspard called Paul to him.

"Paul, boy, you are free to take your way as far as these are concerned. Their way may not be yours. I lay no obligation upon you. This woman is my lawful wife. She is wise and good. But you will do justly by them. This little one," touching the blind girl beside him, "I had hoped might have had her sight restored. Now—" for the first time since his wounding Gaspard showed signs of breaking—"I don't know. Life in the wilds would be hard for her."

"Daddy! Do you think I would leave her?" cried Paul.

"Thank you, Paul! Thank God for you, Paul!" Then the Indian woman at a sign took the children away, leaving Paul close to his bedside.

As the evening fell Gaspard grew rapidly weaker, the doctor relieving as best he could his pain and distress throughout the dreary hours of the night. Then at the breaking of the day his spirit fared forth to meet the dawn.

All through the summer the valley looked on with amazed approval and sympathy at Paul as with a man's wisdom and courage he ran the Pine Croft ranch. Looked on, and more. More than once the neighbours gathered in an old-fashioned bee and helped the boy with the crops, the fencing, the branding of stock and with other ranch operations before which Paul, with his lack of experience and labour, would have been quite helpless. Under the burden of responsibility and of incessant work the boy developed a gravity of demeanour and a strength of purpose far beyond his years. With all childish games and sports he had done. Sleeman, who had disappeared from the valley upon the day of the tragedy, he never saw, but never forgot. Asa he ignored completely and avoided, but Adelina he frequently met in his

lonely rides round the range. Her he found it impossible
to ignore. She would not permit him to do so, and indeed,
after the first shock which the sight of her gave him, Paul
came to tolerate, then to enjoy, her company on those
lonely rides of his. She was a good comrade, a capable
assistant in emergencies and with an amazing endowment
of tact and delicacy of feeling.

At the "big white house" Paul was a welcome and
frequent visitor, but not upon the old footing. His
lessons were done with. He had no time for them, but
more than that he had assumed, with his responsibility
as a man, a man's attitude toward life and a man's
manners. For some weeks Peg openly resented this new
rôle of Paul's, ridiculing it as a thing "put on," a mere
pose. But the boy's gravity and gentleness, his preoccupation in his work and his constant association with
her father and the men effectually shut Peg out from his
life. She found before the summer was over that the
fourteen-year-old boy had in a single day become a man,
and a man to whom she had become a mere child.
She had lost a playmate and had not yet acquired a
friend.

But if she had lost one playmate she gained another,
in the little blind Tanna, who in great measure helped
her to endure her loss and to overcome her resentment.
Through the long summer days Peg found in the little
girl a new and altogether delightful interest. After much
persuasion on Peg's part and after approval by Paul, the
little girl was allowed by her mother to mount old Tubby's
back behind old Tubby's mistress and to take many a
sober jaunt hither and thither along the quiet trails.
Those were golden days for Peg, when Paul could make
it chime with his work to join them in their jaunts or to
meet them at a convenient rendezvous and share their
lunch. With Paul, his very shadow everywhere, went
Peter, a silent, dour, devoted henchman, rejoicing to fetch
and carry for his chief.

The mother, thus left much alone with her grief, withdrew more and more from the life of the household. Like a dark shadow she glided about the house, rarely speaking except to her little blind child, and spending most of her days in the woods near to the enclosed plot on the pine-shadowed hillside where was the new-made grave beside the two others, which held all that had made life for her vivid with love and gladness. Except when spoken to by Paul her face was masked by the passionless colour of the dead. Paul alone could kindle a flicker of light in her sombre eyes and set tremulous life waves rippling over her face. Often she would be found by Paul, wearing her Indian dress and roaming the woods, ostensibly seeking for roots and herbs for medicinal use. It seemed as if her loneliness and grief were driving her away from the newer environment of the white men's civilisation and back to the ancient racial and primeval precincts of her own people.

In late September the word went through the valley that Sleeman had returned and had shut himself up in his ranch, holding communication with none but his own people. That word produced a strange effect upon the Indian woman. The casual mention of Sleeman's name seemed to galvanise into vivid life her dead face. A new gleam appeared in the depths of her sombre eyes and burned there with a steady glow. Her wanderings began to take her to the hills behind the Sleeman ranch. One afternoon, wearied with a long day in the saddle after straying cattle, Paul, allowing his pinto to graze at will, lay down to rest and fell asleep in a thicket. He was startled into wakefulness by the sense of some living thing near him, which becomes second nature with those bred in the wilds. Creeping stealthily toward the edge of the thicket which sheltered him he saw erect upon an out-jutting rock a woman's figure with wind blown tresses, with one hand outstretched toward the Sleeman ranch and in her outstretched hand a long hunting knife. It was the Indian woman Onawata. In the rhythmic cadence of a wailing chant her voice rose and fell, thrilling with suppressed and passionate emotion. The boy shuddered as he listened, but deemed it wisdom to remain hidden from her view. As he lay watching the chanting ceased, the woman fell upon her knees, lifted her face toward the skies, her lips moving as if in prayer, raised high above her head her knife, pressed the naked blade to her lips, made the sign of the cross, bowed her head a few moments as if again in prayer, then rose to her feet and wearily took her way. A weird mingling it was of primal human emotions, expressing themselves in a ritual in which Christian and pagan symbolism found a place. Shocked, startled, terrified, the boy waited a sufficient time to allow her to remove from the vicinity, then mounting his pinto rode hard to the "big white house," where he laid before the Colonel the thing he had seen and heard.

"What does it mean, Paul?" inquired the Colonel when the boy had finished his tale.

"Why, Uncle Colonel, it means only one thing, the thing I would mean if—if—God would let me. But He won't let me. Besides," he added as if to himself, "I promised Daddy."

"You are right, boy. It is not given into our hands to take vengeance. God will——"

"But that's just it, Uncle Colonel. God won't. And——"

"How do you know, boy? Don't you go dictating to the Almighty. He has his own ways and times that to His wisdom seem best. Who are we to instruct Him what to do and when? No, boy, leave the ordering of the universe to God. Do your own work and let God do His. But this thing may lead to some desperate deed."

"Onawata is acting very queerly. She sits for hours under the trees. She eats little food. She gets up at night and wanders round the house. I am awfully afraid she will do something. What can I do?"

"We can only watch her, and do all we can to turn her mind to other things," said the Colonel. "She is very,

very lonely and very sad, and by continual kindness we may help her to forget."

"She will never forget," said Paul.

The very next day Paul was much cheered by the proposal of Onawata that they should all go riding. Immediately he responded to the suggestion. Saddles and bridles were furbished up, with saddle bags for food, and a delightful day was spent by the family, with Peg in charge of little Tanna. This was but the beginning of many such days throughout the golden month of September, and Paul reported to the colonel a most cheering improvement in Onawata's whole bearing.

"That is quite good news. Poor thing! she will soon be all right again. Keep up the riding excursions. Peg is quite delighted. They are doing her as well as Onawata a world of good. Keep 'em up, Paul, keep 'em up. If we could only get her interested in our local social events now it would be a great thing for her. There's our fall picnic now coming off next week. By Jove! I shall speak to Augusta. We must get her out to that, eh? what? Must try to work that, eh?" The Colonel was full of a generous excitement over the prospect.

To his utter surprise and delight Paul found Onawata quite ready to consider the possibility of the picnic, and during the days intervening the whole family was occupied with preparations for the great event. It was no small disappointment to all concerned therefore that on the morning of the picnic day both Peter and Tanna were so completely in the grip of some children's ailment as to be quite unfit to support the excitements of the day. There was nothing for it but that the mother and children should abandon all thought of anything but a perfectly quiet day at home. Paul attached himself to the Colonel's party, and Peg attached herself to Paul. For that day at least Paul appeared to throw off the cares of manhood so prematurely thrust upon him and with Peg abandoned himself to the delights of a boy's holiday. The dark of the evening found two very happy people riding up the lane toward the "big white house."

"It has been a wonderful day, Paul," said Peg, "and you have been just like you used to."

"It's been a jolly day, all right," said Paul. "And I am awfully glad Joseph showed those fellows how to jump."

"And you beat Asa out at the last," exclaimed Peg rapturously. "I think he is just a horrid boy, though he is so big and strong."

"Huh!" grunted Paul.

"Well, he *is* strong, you know, and he is great in football. We never would have beaten the Post but for him."

"Oh, he can play football all right," admitted Paul, with something of a grudge. "He's a little slow, of course, but——"

"But then he is so awfully sure at back. He just tumbled those forwards about. Of course, he spends a lot of time practising."

"Huh!" again grunted Paul.

"You can't really be a good player without practice, can you?"

"Oh, I dunno," said Paul, who had given little attention to football and who in consequence, though giving great promise because of his unusual speed, had not won any great glory on the field that day. "I don't care much for football anyway."

"Oh, Paul, I just love it. It's a wonderful game."

"Oh, pshaw!" said Paul in contempt of a game in which he did not excel.

"Oh, never mind," said Peg cheerfully, "we won the jumps anyway. And Joseph was a regular deer in the racing."

"Wasn't he?" exclaimed Paul, restored to good humour by the remembrance of his pinto's achievements at the picnic, where he won premier honours from the field.

"And, Paul, you were good to me," said Peg shyly when they came to the bars.

"Oh, shucks, Peg!" said Paul, greatly pleased.

"You were, Paul. And that Adelina is just a bold thing."

"Oh, she isn't half bad. Rides awfully well."

"Yes, she does," acknowledged Peg, "but she has a wonderful pony. And don't you think that cap she wore was awfully funny?"

"Why! that's a regular jockey's cap, she told me."

"Jockey cap! For a girl!" Peg's finer sensibilities were obviously offended. She, however, skilfully and lightly turned from distressing and disturbing subjects of conversation to one in which she was more deeply concerned.

"But, Paul, you have never been over at our house once this summer," she said reproachfully, "and you used to come every week at least."

"Why, Peg! I've been often over here."

"Yes, on some old business or other with Daddy."

"Oh! Well!"

"Well! I don't call that anything. You never see me —us, I mean. You never play for us. And you're always so busy. And—and—Paul, you are just forgetting all about us." This was going a long way for the proud-spirited Peggy.

Paul considered a few moments. "Yes! I guess that's so, Peg. But I *am* busy, you know. And besides, they want me at home. They always want me to play for them before going to bed. Their mother used to sing queer little Indian songs about the beasts and the trees and the stars and things. And then I spin them out on the piano, you know. And the little one, she's just wild over them and—you know—it is awfully hard for her, always in the dark—Oh, Peg, no light! It must be just terrible for her!"

"I know, I know, Paul. You are just a dear to poor little Tanna. Oh, it is so awfully sad for her. And I am a pig to want you to come away from her."

"You're not a pig, Peg," said Paul indignantly. "You

are just fine to Tanna, and I won't ever forget that, Peggy."

They had turned Tubby out into the paddock and were standing in the soft light of the September moon near the corral. Peg's voice grew very soft as she answered, "But I just love her, Paul, and I want to be good to her because I'm sorry for her—and—and because she is your sister. She *is,* isn't she, Paul?" Peg finished a little breathlessly.

Paul turned this over in his mind. He was conscious of queer stirrings within him. It came to him all at once that Peg was a girl, not simply a fine and splendid chum, but something different from himself. The moonlight fell in a soft glory upon her sweet face and dainty girlish figure. As he stood looking at her she smiled up into his face. A warm rush of something, he knew not what, filled his whole body from his toes upward.

"Peggy," he said with a quick catch in his breath, "I think—I'd like to kiss you."

The little girl's eyes grew large with something almost like fear, but she did not shrink away from him. Instead she lifted up her face, smiling with tremulous lips.

"Would you, Paul?" she said.

He suddenly caught her in his arms and kissed her.

"Oh, Paul, that was my nose," said Peg in a disappointed voice.

"I was in a hurry," explained Paul.

"Why hurry?" inquired Peg innocently.

"That's so," agreed Paul, amazed at her self-command, and then took his time.

It seemed to Paul that he had done a thing immensely significant. Again he looked at Peg and wondered what had happened to her, she was so utterly different; and to himself, he seemed another being. As he continued looking at her he felt no desire to kiss her again. He wondered, indeed, how he had ever come to do such a thing. He wanted rather to protect her. She seemed so little, so tender, so needing protection. It suddenly came to him that henceforth he would always have to stand between her and any harm. She was in his charge, just as Tanna was, and yet with a difference. Yes, a wonderful and delightful difference. He was greatly puzzled over it all. He wanted to get away alone and think.

"Good night, Peg," he said abruptly, and swung himself on his pinto.

"Good night, Paul," answered Peg in a voice shy and tender. Something in her tone set Paul's nerves tingling again. He wanted to get off his horse and kiss her again, but somehow he felt too that this would not be fair to her. She looked so little, so unprotected. No, he must not do it.

"Good night, Peg. I'll see you tomorrow. It's been a wonderful day, Peggy."

"Oh, wonderful, Paul! I won't ever forget!" sighed Peg, looking so sweet, so wistful, so radiant in the moonlight that Paul, feeling his control threatened by the surge of strange emotions, dug his heel into the pinto and swung him down the lane at a gallop.

Peg stood motionless, watching till she saw him clear the bars, then listened so long as she could hear the pony's hoof beats drumming far up the road. Then she drew a long breath, gazed round about her as if upon a strange world and smiled up at the moon in a friendly way as if sharing with the man there a delicious secret. Then she put her fingers softly to her lips, looked at them, kissed them gently and went quietly into the house and soon to bed, a happy-hearted if somewhat bewildered little girl. And over all the world the moon rode high, serene in her soft and radiant splendour.

Within an hour there came to Peg up in her bedroom the sound again of hoof beats, hard driven as by dread of impending death. Nearer they came and nearer and with no slackening speed. She sprang to the window. She heard her father go to the door. She could make out the piebald coat of the pinto coming down the lane.

Clearing the bars in his stride the pinto came with unchecked speed to the very door. From the saddle Paul hurled himself and fell breathless in the Colonel's arms.

"Oh! Uncle Colonel!" he gasped. "She's—done it!"

"Steady, boy. Steady, Paul. Wait! Not a word," commanded the Colonel, holding the boy with steady hands. "Wait! Not a word! Take your time! Sixty of a count!" The Colonel proceeded quietly counting while Paul, to whom this law of the Colonel was well known to be inexorable, got his breath and quieted his nerves.

"Now then, quietly, Paul! Go on!" said the Colonel in a voice peremptory and calm.

"Uncle Colonel, you see that light beyond the hill? That's Sleeman's house. She—Onawata has killed him with her knife and then set fire to the house. I found her all ready to go, with horses saddled and packs made up. They have gone."

"Who?" said the Colonel sharply.

"Onawata and Peter and—and Tanna. And I——"

"Where have they gone?"

"Colonel, I don't think I ought to tell you. You see, the police will be after them. And I am going too."

"You, Paul? Nonsense! You must not think of such a thing."

"Uncle Colonel, I must go with them. I see that to be right. I promised Daddy to care for them. And there's Tanna——"

"Nonsense, Paul! Let them go! They don't need you. You can't throw away your life like that. Anyway they will be caught. You must not mix up yourself with this thing."

"I must go, Uncle Colonel. I could not go without seeing you. I must go! Oh! I must go! I promised Daddy! And Tanna will need me. Good-bye—good-bye!" He caught his reins preparatory to mounting.

"But, good God, Paul! You see what this means? Don't you see that——"

"Colonel Pelham," said Paul quietly, "I see it clearly.

That's why I must go. God wants me to." The Colonel knew the boy well enough to realise the utter finality of his resolve.

"Well, Paul, God keep you, boy, if you must go. God keep you, my dear boy."

"He will, Uncle Colonel. I know He will. And some day I'll come back. Say good-bye to Peg. Tell her I'll never forget." The boy was speaking in the voice and manner of a full grown man, and like a man the Colonel treated him. He would fain have taken the lad in his arms, for he loved him as if he had been his own son, but somehow the grave, firm tones, the steady voice, checked any demonstration. They shook hands in farewell and Paul swung himself onto the pinto. But before he could turn his pony round a little white figure appeared at the door, and with a faint cry ran toward him with hands outstretched.

"Paul! Paul! You are going away! I know! I heard!"

Flinging himself from the saddle Paul was at her side, and holding her hands in his stood silent, fighting to hold himself steady.

"You are going away, Paul!" Again came the pitiful cry.

"Oh, Peggy! dear Peggy! I must go, I must go. Uncle Colonel, take her away, take her away. Good-bye, Peggy."

Her father touched her arm. "Come, Peggy," he said quietly. "Paul must go."

"Daddy! Daddy!" she cried. "He'll never come back!"

"Peggy, listen to me," said the boy, once more speaking in a man's voice. "I shall come back to you. Remember what I say. And, Uncle Colonel, you remember too, I am coming back. And, Peggy, I'll never, never forget." He turned once more to mount.

"Paul," the child's voice was sharp with grief, "you didn't—say—good-bye."

The boy stood hesitating, then came to the Colonel. His man's pose fell from him.

"Uncle Colonel," he said, his voice quivering pitifully, "good-bye." He put out his arms, the Colonel drew him to his breast and kissed him on the cheek twice.

"Good-bye, my boy. The good God have you in His care."

"Good-bye, Peggy," said Paul, and putting his arms round her kissed her on the lips.

"Good-bye! dear, dear Paul," whispered Peggy, clinging to him. "I won't ever forget."

In her father's arms she lay listening while the hoof beats drummed farewell far down the trail and faded into silence.

CHAPTER XV

A white plain swept by furious winds and fit for the foot of God, white with a dazzling whiteness except where the red sun half down the western slope touched the wind-ruffled snowdrifts with a burnish of gold, gold deepening to purple in the hollows: a pitiless plain, glaring white up to a pitiless sky glaring blue and a pitiless sun glaring red, blinding the eyes, and swept by a wind, a pitiless wind that cut through fur coverings clean to the bone and reached with icy edge to the very heart. Across this pitiless, glaring, wind-swept, sun-burnished plain now a little party made its painful way; a youth verging to full manhood; a boy in his early teens; a girl some years his junior, a mere child indeed; fur-clad all of them, leading and driving three limping dogs attached to a toboggan. Upon the toboggan lay a woman wrapped close in furs. Where the drifts obscured the trail the youth broke the way for the team of limping dogs which the boy following lashed into movement lest they should drop in their tracks. Led by a dog trace behind the toboggan, the little girl ran lightly and easily through the broken snow or over the hardened crust, the freshest of the party. Wrapped to the eyes in furs they could defy the knife-edged wind just so long as they kept in motion. Halt they dared not, for death, hard and close upon their tracks, haunted their trail.

Breaking the track and pulling hard on his leading line, the young man, with unseeing eyes set in his haggard face, strode, or rather stumbled along, leaning far over his stride like one ever on the verge of falling. For the last hour and more he had abandoned any attempt to hold the trail. The main direction he knew lay down this frozen lake, and between the flanking lines of low bush half a

171

mile distant on either side. Half a day's journey away was the Hudson's Bay Post, the last lap in their fifteen days' struggle against wind and sun and snow-blocked trail. A struggle it was of growing desperation. For the first three days of their journey they knocked off their twenty miles a day, all four running lightly. Then a three days' blizzard held them fast, with their grub sack growing lighter. For the next four days the best that was in them could cover a bare ten miles a day, for the woman whose feverish eagerness had driven them through the last weary miles of every day's run, had fallen in her tracks and against fierce protestations had been forced to the toboggan. Again a blizzard of three days brought them to starvation rations, with still thirty-five miles between them and safety. The night before the woman had converse with the young man.

"Paul, you will need to do the driving now," said the woman. "I can no longer. We must make the Post, Paul. Why not take the children with you and leave me in camp here? You can run swiftly and come back for me. I don't wish to be the death of all of you. It is I that have been a curse to you and your family from the first. Oh, if I could pay the price by dying now!"

"Onawata, you are always wise, but tonight you are not wise. I might go through alone and bring you help, but we shall try one day more. At any cost we must stick together."

"One day more then, Paul," replied Onawata, "but promise me you will not sacrifice the living to the dying."

"Dying? Wait till we get you to a doctor. We will make a good run tomorrow."

"You will not promise? There is Tanna."

"God means us to go through. I know He does." The Calvinist in him forbade despair. He had the sense of being somehow included in the plan of the eternal decrees. Nothing could kill that conviction. And hence he would, he must follow his gleam so far as it led.

"Promise me, Paul," pleaded the Indian woman with

passionate intensity. "Death has spoken to me. I have heard his voice. Soon, soon, a few weeks at most, I go with him. Why should the young die for me?"

"I promise to do the best for them," said Paul solemnly.

"And if the choice comes at last you will choose that they shall live?"

"Yes, I will promise."

"Good! You will not fail. You have never been anything but true, Paul. Your God will not fail you."

"Your God, too, Onawata," said Paul gently.

"Ah, there is only One—the Great Spirit, the Great Father. Perhaps He will let a poor and evil child creep in at His feet. Ah-yah-i-yah—" wailed the woman. "The light had gone out, the dark filled my soul, I saw no way, I made my way, it was the way of death, death to him also who deserved death, and death to me—and death—ah-yah-i-yah—death to all I love—perhaps——"

"Hush, hush, Mammy!" said Paul, soothing her as he might a child. "God is good, He forgives, He forgives. Never fear Him. And I know we shall get through. Now rest. We start again at dawn."

The next day a driving head wind and the blinding drift slowed down the pace of the limping dogs to a bare ten miles for the five hours of daylight, leaving twenty-five miles still to go.

Again the Indian woman besought Paul to try the journey with a light toboggan and the children and leave her in camp.

"They will not hinder you much, Paul. Even Tanna can keep up with you. But I drag you down to death." But Paul could not be persuaded.

"One day more," he said. "Then if I must I will."

But next morning the tail of a blizzard held them fast for two precious hours. One of the dogs refused to move and Paul with a swift blow of the hatchet put it out of misery and fed the emaciated bones to the others. After that Onawata had surreptitiously, when the others were after wood, saved some fragments of the flesh. When the blizzard had somewhat broken, Paul once more got the little party on the march, Onawata marching with the rest. An hour's run however found her staggering with pain and weakness, and Paul forced her to the toboggan.

"We shall make it tonight," he said. "It is going to be fine now." But the woman shook her head.

"No, no," she said. "There is another storm coming."

"Not a bit of it," declared Paul. "Look at that sky."

"Hurry! hurry!" said the woman.

For another two hours Paul led the way, breaking the crusted trail, ploughing his way through drifts and dragging his limping team and part of their load after him. The wind had dropped, and with it the temperature. The icy cold fell upon them, its penetrating thrust making for heart, lungs and every vital organ. Pause they dared not. In the lead, Paul, staggering forward with legs numb from sheer weariness and lessening vitality, broke the trail for the dogs, leaning his weight hard upon his leading line. Behind the toboggan the boy lashed the crawling dogs with weird Indian objurgations, behind him again the little blind girl, guided by a dog trace, ran lightly over the broken trail, her spirit still undaunted.

A deeper drift than usual halted the party till Paul should break a way for the bleeding feet of the dogs. At the pause the dogs fell prone in the snow, panting and whimpering. The boy at the rear of the toboggan dropped upon his knees and fell huddled on his face. Looking back, Paul saw him thus huddled in the snow. With a loud harsh cry he staggered back, seized the boy by the neck and shoulder, shook him with savage fury, cuffed him, kicked him up onto his legs. Peter stood swaying on his feet, looked about him with a dazed, sickly grin upon his face.

"What's the matter? Was I asleep long?" he asked thickly.

"Asleep long? Asleep long? You blasted idiot! Don't you know what sleep means on this trail? Nice man you are on a job like this!"

Slowly into the dark face of the boy the red blood came up, then, ebbing, left it grey.

"All right, Chief," he muttered, "I sleep no more."

"Listen to me, Peter. If you ever drop again I'll cut you to pieces with your dog whip."

Peter gazed, dumb and shuddering, at his chief, as he called him; not that he feared the whip, but because in all his life he had never heard Paul speak to him in such a tone.

"We are going through, and no one must drop or stop. We must get through! We must get through! And, by the Eternal God," he lifted his clenched fists toward the hard, pitiless blue sky, "we will go through!" At the terrible furious voice the little girl began to cry. Paul glared at her a moment or two. Never in his life had he been so near breaking.

"Stop it!" he snarled, baring his teeth like a dog.

"Yes, Paul, I'll stop," said the child, her quivering lips setting in a firm line. His eyes softened as he looked upon her.

"All right, Tanna. *You* won't quit," he said.

Once more, under the emphasis, the red flushed up in the face of the boy.

"Who's a-quittin'?" he said angrily.

"Get your dogs going," replied Paul, picking up his line. But neither commands nor lashings could move the leader from the snowdrift where he lay. With a low exclamation of fury Paul stepped to the toboggan.

"We can't fool with you," he said, fumbling among the camp stuff.

"What is it?" cried the girl. "Which dog?"

"Lynx," said the boy in a low voice.

With a little cry, "Paul, don't!" she sprang forward, stumbled over the toboggan, scrambled to her feet, felt her way over the dog team till she came to the leader, then kneeling down beside him she put her arms round the grizzled husky.

"Oh, Lynx," she murmured in his ear, "good Lynx,

dear Lynx, try once more, Lynx." The dog whined, licked the face bending over him, struggled to his feet. "He will go now, Paul," she said eagerly. "He will try again. See!" She caught the dog by the collar. "Come on, Lynx. Come, Bliz. Come, good dogs. Hup! hup! mush! mush!" The three dogs strained on their collars, swaying on the traces, a shout, a plunge, and the toboggan stood free from the drift. Paul replaced the axe in the camp kit.

"He has saved himself this time," he muttered. "Get to your place, Tanna." The girl with a loud cheery cry called again to the dogs, her hand on the head of the leader. Once more with a whine they responded and the toboggan was on its way again over the crusted snow.

"Now then, a little run here, the going is good," cried Paul, picking up his lead line. But the woman's voice stayed him.

"Wait, Paul," she said, raising herself on her elbow. She pushed the hood back from her face and gazed about her at sky and woods. "No, Paul, we shall make camp," she said. "A storm is coming." She pointed to the angry sun and the four brilliant sun-dogs surrounding it. "We must make camp, Paul, and quick. Look! There is good wood." She pointed to a thick clump of pines and underbrush at the edge of the lake. The young man growled impatiently.

"We can make it," he said in a voice of sullen desperation. "How far is the Post yet?" She held up her two hands twice. "Twenty miles yet!" he exclaimed in dismay. "We could make it before morning," he added stubbornly.

"Yes, if the storm kept off and if I could walk," said the woman, a bitter weariness in her voice.

Quickly Paul surrendered. "We will camp," he said, swinging off toward the bushy pine bluff. "Come on, Lynx, you!" With a glad whimper the dogs strained on their traces and set off on a limping gallop. They knew

as well as any that the welcome camp ground lay before
them.

In among the thick undergrowth of scrub pine they
dragged the toboggan where they found shelter from the
cutting wind.

"Lie where you are, Mammy," said Paul. "We will
have a fire in a minute or two." The woman turned over
with a groan.

"Is it very bad, Mammy?" said the little girl, kneeling
down beside the toboggan.

"The pain? That matters not," said the woman bitterly. "It is hard to drag you all back, perhaps to——"
she paused abruptly.

"Everybody at work!" shouted Paul, seizing the axe
and slashing down with swift, sure blows the young spruce
and balsams, and flinging them in a heap near the toboggan. Swiftly the little girl fell upon them with a long
hunting knife, slicing off the boughs for the bed.

"The fire, Peter!" snapped Paul. "Jump!" Peter
needed no urging. With eager intensity they all flung
themselves at their work, the bed, the fire, the supper,
wood for the night, and a shelter against the impending
storm. It was a race for life with the swift-coming night,
for night finding them unprepared meant death to some
of them, perhaps to all. They each knew their special
tasks and with swift despatch they went at their work.
While Paul was slashing down the underbrush, Peter
having gathered a large pile of dry brushwood was digging
out with a frying pan a large circular space some seven
feet in diameter. This done he proceeded to pile his
brushwood in the circular space he had cleared, and soon
he had a fire blazing under which the snow rapidly melted
away. Then, seizing the axe which Paul had laid aside,
he went off for more wood. There could not be too
much wood with a storm blowing up, for if the storm
became a blizzard wood meant life. Meantime, with
saplings stripped bare of their branches and the trees
standing thick about, Paul was constructing a shelter as

near the fire as was safe, weaving the branches thatchwise till a fairly thick semi-circular brushwood wall stood about the fire. Around this shelter he would stretch later a strip of canvas and some soft deer skins which were still in the toboggan. An hour's strenuous work saw a crude but fairly substantial brushwood built on three sides of the deep circular hollow from which the fire had partially melted the snow. Clearing from this hollow space the melted slush Paul proceeded to bank the sides high with the softened snow which almost immediately was frozen into a solid mass impervious to wind. Upon the space thus cleared, he placed a thick layer of balsam boughs. These he covered over with a fur rug.

"Now, Mammy! There you are!" he cried cheerily. "In you go. We will have supper in no time."

Painfully the woman dragged herself out of the toboggan and seated herself in the shelter.

"Now, then, Tanna, you have the water ready?"

"Soon, Paul, I think," said the child, who had meantime been nursing a small fire under a pail of melted snow. "You go for the wood," she added, "we can do the rest."

"Look out for the fire then," said Paul.

"I will watch her," said the woman. "You can go for the wood. Get plenty; we may need much."

"You need not fear for me," said the girl. "I have no eyes in my head, but my fingers are as good as eyes." For a few moments Paul stood watching.

"Yes! You are a wonder, little one," he said in a low voice, touched with pity.

The girl lifted her face to him, showing two large blue eyes whose lustre was dimmed with a scarcely perceptible film. But though the blue of the eye was somewhat dimmed the spirit that shone through the face was one of untamed invincibility.

"Go, Paul," said the woman. "She is quite safe." She paused, then added with infinite sadness in her voice, "While she has me she is safe."

The girl felt her way to the woman and passed her hands over her face. "Do not fear for me, Mammy. I shall take great care." The woman took the child in her arms and, rocking herself to and fro, held her there in a passionate embrace. The young man turned hastily away on his quest for dry wood, for already the sun had finished his brief winter course and with dying rays was glaring angrily at the swiftly triumphing night.

The evening meal consisted of a watery stew, the nourishing ingredients of which were a pork rind, the last remnant of their meat supply, some fragments of hard tack, and some spare bones with dark red ragged remnants of flesh attached, which the woman had thrown into the pot but as to the nature of which none of them made inquiry. In other circumstances, Paul at least would have turned with loathing from the revolting mess, but tonight he forced himself to devour with ravenous haste the portion assigned him by the woman. Eat he must if he were to carry his party through the last twenty miles.

The sick woman ate a morsel of food, drank a little of the soup, then, gripped with agonising pains, refused further nourishment.

Some bones saved from the last camp were thrown to the dogs who with much savage snarling and fighting soon cleared them away.

The fire, originally laid upon a foundation of green spruce logs and now burned down to glowing embers, was drawn almost within the enclosure of the shelter and kept alive with judicious care. Within the recesses of the shelter the party disposed themselves for the night. The girl crept within the woman's fur rug and soon fell asleep. The boy huddled close beside them and, as near the fire as he dared, sat fighting off the overpowering drowsiness that threatened every moment to subdue him.

"You go to sleep, Peter," said Paul. "I'll take the first watch. I'll promise to wake you."

"Word of honour?" said the boy.

"Word of honour!" replied Paul.

The boy sat a little longer, then reluctantly snuggled down among the brush and instantly sank into a dead sleep.

With the night the threatening storm came howling down upon the little company, hissing, moaning, shrieking, as if legions of demons were riding the winds, destruction in their hearts. Around their frail structure the blizzard piled up a great bank of snow, effectually shutting out the piercing wind, so that with the heat from the glowing fire in front the sleepers took no hurt from the Arctic cold. The chief danger lay in the blizzard. Alone Paul might buck through, but with the sick woman and the little blind girl the attempt would be worse than madness. The blizzard might last for three days, even for five, and they were at the end of their food. Spent though he was with his two weeks' fight against head winds and drifts through the long and terrible miles, his gnawing anxiety for the little company dependent upon him had worn his nerves so ragged and raw that Paul felt no need of sleep, as the slow hours of the night dragged out their weary length. Never had he been more wide awake, more keenly sensitive to the terrors and dangers of his environment. He found himself listening and trying to differentiate the voices of the storm outside. Through the birches and poplars, bare of leaf, the blasts rattled and hissed like nests of serpents; through the spruce and pine they moaned and sighed like souls in distress. As he sat listening to the mingling voices of the blizzard he began to hear in them the notes of hate and savage fury as of raging beasts. The woods seemed to be filled with them. He shivered, listening to shriekings and howlings, low snarls and growls, cries and weird callings of beasts he had never known, and all the northern beasts he knew well for he had hunted them to their dens and holes. He seemed to catch a note of triumph, of savage exultant triumph, through the tumult. They had him sure and fast. They knew it and he began to fear it. They seemed to be closing in upon him. He could hear beneath the howlings and shriekings the hiss of their whispering voices just at the back of the shelter. He sprang to his feet. He would meet them out there on their own ground. Out from the cover of the shelter he leaped into the blizzard. The cutting drive of the granulated snow bit into his bare face. A moment he stood staring into the blinding, cutting, needle-pointed drift, then suddenly he stumbled back and sank huddled behind the shelter, his soul and body shaken by the impact of a new fear. Was he going mad? It was no unknown thing in those terror ridden wilds for strong men to be driven mad. Huddled and shaking he sat straining his ears after the voices daring him forth. Then to him thus straining, with every nerve taut and every sense a-tingle, there came through the raging, shrieking, hissing welter a voice clear as the song of a bird in the stillness of the dawn, a voice clear and familiar:

"He maketh the clouds His chariot, He walketh upon the wings of the wind."

A wonderful quiet fell upon him. In the clear warm glow of the firelight in the old Pine Croft bungalow he saw a boy sitting on a low stool, gazing up into a face alight with serene courage. Outside, the tempest howled down the valley, lashing the windows, pounding at the doors and twisting the huge pines about like wisps of hay.

"That is a good verse to learn tonight, my boy," the woman was saying. And over and over again, till the words were bedded firmly in his soul, she chanted the great words of that noble Hebrew psalm.

As on that night long ago, so tonight again the storm suddenly lost its power to terrify him. He remembered the vision he had that night of the great God out there, the good and kindly God whom he had been taught to know as his friend, riding forth down the Windermere upon his rolling cloud chariot and borne upon the wings of the wind. Gone was his paralysing fear. He rose from his huddled position and stood at the mouth of the shelter, his own man again. Steadily he faced the howling blizzard.

It had lost its terror. He raised his hand high above his head, as if in salute. He knew he was not alone. He would win through. Deep in his soul was the conviction whose roots ran far back into his childhood memories, that in the eternal covenant and plan his life had a place. That, among others, he owed to his mother. Yes, he would win through. No blizzards that blew could down him. His Calvinistic faith held him steady on his course.

He threw some wood on the fire and as the wood crackled up he touched Peter on the arm. Instantly the boy was wide awake.

"Quiet!" whispered Paul. The dark Indian face immediately hardened into bronze, the black eyes only gleaming with life.

"Come," signalled Paul.

Carefully the boy stepped around the fire and sat down beside his brother. Upon a piece of birch bark, with a burnt stick, Paul drew an outline of the lake, showing the trail leading to the Hudson's Bay Post at the south-east end, as he had got it from Onawata.

"Peter, I am going to the Post tonight. You stay here. Keep the fire going. Some one will come for you. Keep the fire going and make a big smoke all the time. Kill the dogs if you must."

"Wait for the morning, eh?" he said, his dark eyes imploring.

"No, I must get through. The blizzard may last three days, then it will be too late for any of us. You see?" The boy nodded silent assent.

"When the fire burns low twice wake me up." Again the boy nodded.

"Good boy! We'll get through," said Paul, putting his hand on his shoulder. The boy's face flushed red, then grew grey again. The chances for getting through he knew well were very slim indeed.

With but a moment's further delay Paul lay down near the fire. Round the little snow-banked shelter the storm howled its wildest, but through all its strident and threatening voices another voice came, calm and serene and heart-stilling, "He rideth upon the wings of the wind," and Paul hearing that voice was instantly asleep.

CHAPTER XVI

The Hudson's Bay Post stood at the southern end of the lake, as did most Hudson's Bay Posts in the North Country, and consisted of a group of log buildings, well constructed, neat in appearance and well adapted to their purposes of trade and defence. The store, with the Factor's house attached, was the most imposing of the group, and next in size was the Mission House, which did for dwelling for the missionary, the church and the school, all under one roof and within four walls. Straggling outhouses were scattered about where boats and canoes and tackle of different kinds were stored. A few Indian wigwams and well built huts near the forest line completed the picture.

It was early morning and the air was bitter cold and thick with driving snow. About the Post there was not a sign of life except at the door of the Mission House, where a six-dog team hitched to a toboggan waited for their master. In their harness they lay curled up, backs to the wind, a nondescript lot, of varied and altogether doubtful ancestry but mostly husky.

Suddenly the leader raised his head, pricked up his ears, sniffed the wind and uttered a short sharp bark. Instantly the remaining five were on their feet, vigorously barking, indignant that they had missed something and protesting that they knew quite as much as old Skookum, who after his first warning bark had remained standing stiff-legged and bristled as to his back, sniffing the wind. The door of the Mission House opened and a little man, fur-clad as for a journey, looked out.

"What's up, Skookum? Lie down, you old idiot," he said. The other five looked foolish, but old Skookum maintained his posture, with ears alert and hair stiff and bristling. He knew that down the wind a definite and authentic scent had struck his nostrils. His was no second-hand knowledge, and he was not to be browbeaten into denial of a veritable experience.

"Well, old son, you are not usually an ass," said the missionary. "We will investigate."

He ran down to the shore and looked up the lake through the drifting snow. "Nothing there," he muttered, "but Skookum knows a thing or two." Long and steadily he gazed, waiting for a break in the drift of snow.

"By Jove! I believe there is something moving out there," he said. Long he stood peering through the breaking drift that blinded his eyes and for the most part shut out the landscape. But nothing was to be seen. He returned to the house.

"You smelt something, old boy," he said, patting the leader's head, "but it's gone away. A fox or something, eh?" But Skookum's nose was still in the air and he refused to accept anything but the testimony of that reliable organ. As the missionary turned to re-enter the house Skookum again lifted his voice in a sharp, decisive bark and again his chorus supported him with vociferous yelping.

"Shut up, you idiots," said the man to the five chorus dogs. "You didn't smell anything." For a moment the missionary stood undecided, looking at Skookum. "All right, old boy. It's a beastly day to be out in, too beastly to take a chance. We'll take your word for it."

He entered the house, shouting, "Mother, Skookum says there's some one up the lake, so before I go to Pine Point I shall run up a bit."

"All right, John. It is a dreadful storm, but you were going out anyway, and it may be a runner from the Indian camp, you know."

"You're right, Mother, as you always are. I didn't think of that. My mitts? Ah, here they are. And my bottle in case———? Ah, yes, thanks. I shall come in before I start for the Point if I don't find anything. Good-bye."

His wife followed him to the door. "What a day! No! No! Come back, children, from the storm." She drew back into the cosy room two brown-faced little boys who were keen to follow their father to the lake shore.

Within twenty minutes they heard the barking of the dogs, and in another moment her husband burst into the room, steadying a tall slight youth who swayed, staggered, clutched at the door and so hung, his chin fallen on his breast, his breath coming in gasps and deep drawn sobs.

"Quick, Mother, tea!" said the missionary, holding the stranger from falling.

"Here, old chap, sit down. You're all right now," said the missionary, pushing a chair toward him. But the youth clung fast to the door.

"No!" he gasped. "No! Mustn't sit. Mother—two kids—up lake—mustn't sit—never get up again." But even as he spoke his hold loosened on the door. The warm air of the room relaxed his nerve tension and he slumped down in a huddled heap on the floor. Swiftly the missionary's fingers were at work, loosening hood and coat.

"Yes, that's right, Mother," he said, taking from her hand a cup in which she had poured some spirits and hot water. "Now, get this into you. Good! A little more! Ah, now you are coming round. Now finish up the cup. Down with it, do you hear! No nonsense! Fine! Now, let's see how you are. Hands all right, or nearly so. Off with his moccasins, Mother! Feet? Toes frozen a bit. Some snow, Mother, and rub 'em hard. All right, boy! You're sound outside."

So working swiftly he kept up in a loud, cheery voice, now soothing, again commanding, a monologue with which he strove to divert his patient from his own condition and restore him to normal self-control.

"'Now the tea, Mother. A little spirits in it—ah, not

too much—he doesn't need it. Nothing like tea. Puts heart into a man—no unpleasant reactions. Great stuff, tea, for this country, eh? Something to chew on now, Mother. Toast? Nothing better! A little more now. Lots of time though, no rush. Sit down, old chap." By this time the young man was on a chair. "Sit down. *Sit down.* What?"

"No!" said the young man, getting to his feet. "I will not sit! Must get back—mother—two children—in camp—snow bound—starving—dying! Must go." He was on his feet now, his hands stretched out imploringly.

"What?" shouted the missionary. "A woman and children? For God's dear sake, where? How far?"

"Left there—an hour after midnight. Come! She is dying!"

"Where, boy? For God's sake, where?" Without waiting his answer the missionary flung open the door, whistled a succession of shrill blasts with his fingers, waved violently to a man who appeared at the door of one of the huts near by and turned back to the boy.

"What's your name, boy?" he shouted.

"My name? Paul."

"And the woman—your mother?"

"No—yes—my step-mother."

"And dying? Where? Show me!" The missionary dragged him to a map hanging on the wall. The boy shook his head.

"Give me paper," he said.

The missionary thrust paper and pencil into his hands. With shaking fingers he drew a rough outline of the lake, and traced a trail along the east shore.

"There!" he said, indicating a jutting point. "Twenty miles—one hour after midnight—I left."

"Twenty miles! God help us now!" muttered the missionary, making swift preparations. "Quick, Mother! Tea, hot bricks, blankets, grub, whiskey. Ah! Thomas, good man—" he turned to an Indian who had come in— "party lost up the lake, twenty miles. Get ready to go

with me. Another team—the Factor's. Quick! quick!"
Without a word the Indian vanished.

The missionary turned to the boy. "Now, lad, you go
to bed. Mother will look after you." He turned to his
wife, busy with the preparation of food. "Feed him,
Mother, and let him sleep. I know that point. We will
bring them in safe enough."

"I am going. I am all right now," said Paul, pulling
on his moccasins. "I am going. I know the way."

"Nonsense!" shouted the missionary. "You stay here.
You don't go a foot. You will only keep us back."

Paul looked at him stupidly, then smiled. "I am going.
You can't keep me here. I am going." His voice remained quite quiet. "I'll not hold you back. Let me go!
Oh, let me go!" Again his hands went out in an imploring gesture.

The missionary paused in his preparations, keenly
searching the boy's face.

"All right, you young mule!" he snapped. "We haven't
time to argue. Anyway we have two toboggans," he
added to himself. "All right, all right. Feed this youth,
Mother. He can stand some meat now. Fill the beggar
up while we get ready. Here, off with those socks of
yours," he continued. "Dry socks, Mother. Two pairs.
My mackinaws—find a pair of mitts. All right, now!
Steady all!"

His wife, without a word and with swift hands that
never hesitated or fumbled, followed out his instructions.

"Here, boy!" said the missionary. "If you are going
with me, listen and obey orders." There was no mis-
taking that tone.

"Yes, sir, I will!" said Paul. "Tell me what to do."

"First sit here close to the fire," said the missionary,
drawing close to the glowing stove a big rocking chair.
"Eat and drink all you can. Don't guzzle; take your
time. Get dry, warm things on your feet and hands.
We shall not move for twenty minutes or so. Eat—
drink—rest. Do you hear?"

"Yes, sir. I will. I am all right, sir, thank you, sir."

"Good boy! Good stuff, eh? Now don't talk."

Eagerly, ravenously, yet with no indecent haste, he ate the food given him, helping it down with cups of strong tea, pulling on the while dry clothing. Having eaten and got into dry things, he settled himself down into the big rocker. In a dozen breaths he was asleep, insensible, immovable, dead to his world.

The missionary smiled. "We will give him half an hour, Mother. He is dead beat."

"Poor lad! How thin he is! And how terribly worn he looks! I am quite anxious about him, John. He can never go with you. Why not slip away now? You would be back before he wakes."

"He has had a hard go, but he looks fit enough."

"Why not let him sleep? He cannot go twenty miles."

"We will give him half an hour. If he woke and found us gone you would have to tie him. He would follow us till he dropped."

In consultation with Thomas the missionary studied the boy's rough sketch.

"That is just beyond the Petite Traverse, Thomas, eh?"

Thomas pondered. "How long he marshe?"

"From midnight. But he could not make good time in his condition and against that storm, eh?"

Thomas stood calculating. "La Petite Traverse ten miles," he said, holding up two hands. "La Grande Traverse, he—" he showed fifteen fingers "and some more. S'pose he run queeck, eh? No dreeft. De win'—she's blow heem—poof!"

"The Big Traverse!" exclaimed the missionary. "That's good eighteen miles! Still, as you say, there would be little drifting on the lake with this wind. He might do it. By Jove! Thomas, we have a big job before us. And that boy wants to come with us."

"Non, non, he cannot! Impossible!" Thomas was very emphatic, the missionary's wife equally so.

"Look at him, John! Did you ever see a boy so terribly worn?"

The missionary sat regarding the youth. "He is thin and worn. I am sorry I gave him my word, by Jove! Everything ready, Thomas? What have you, Mother? There is a sick woman, you know."

"Starving and worn out, like enough," replied his wife. "There's a bottle of soup and tea and hard tack and meat."

"Fine. We will give him a full half hour."

"Perhaps when he wakes he can be persuaded to wait here," said his wife.

"Not he! He is a mule, a perfect mule. Look at that mouth, that long jaw. He will try it anyway. We may have to put him on the toboggan, but he will go."

Thomas shook his head. "No bon! No bon! Him sleep so five hour, dead like one bear. We go toute suite!"

But to this the missionary would not agree. "At any rate, we must give him the chance to say."

"It's a shame! a crime!" said his wife.

At the end of three-quarters of an hour the missionary stood up, put his hand on the shoulder of the sleeping boy and gave him a slight shake. With one movement the boy was on his feet, awake and alert.

"What is it, Peter? Time, eh?" he asked, gazing upon the faces about him. "I was—I'm afraid I was asleep," he said shamefacedly. "All ready? Let us go." He drew on his light fur coat, seized his mitts, caps and snowshoes.

"No use, Mother," said the missionary. "All right, we're off. You'll see us when we get back. Good-bye." He kissed his wife.

"Oh, he cannot make that trip, John. He will perish on the way," said his wife, quick tears coming to her eyes.

"Nonsense, Mother! He has two days' march in him."

The boy stood, his big grey eyes turning from one to the other. They were concerned for him. The tears in the woman's eyes were for him. Slowly a deep red flush overspread his thin haggard face. Silently he took her hand in both of his, held it for a moment, then with a kind of shy grace he kissed it.

"You are awfully good," he muttered, turned away and made for the door.

"*En avant!*" shouted the missionary cheerily. "All aboard! See you later, Mother!"

There was little breaking trail for the dogs that day; for, in Thomas' dramatic words, "de win' she's blow heem —poof!" So after the first half hour the party struck and held to the steady dog trot that devours the white miles in the north land and keeps the blood jumping in the teeth of forty below. The boy took his turn with the other two in leading. After two hours' run the missionary would have swung off to a bold out-jutting headland, heavily wooded, dimly seen through the storm.

"There is the point beyond the Petite Traverse, Thomas," he said.

"Oui!"

"No, that is not the camp," said Paul. "Farther up, farther up."

"Beyond the Grande Traverse, Thomas, eh?" said the missionary. "Another eight miles at least. Are you fit? Can you go on?"

The boy looked at him a moment with eyes that burned in their deep sockets like points of fire, then without answer he set off on a dog trot on the northward trail.

A twenty minute run brought them round the headland. They were on the edge of the Big Traverse, a bleak white plain, bare of mark or guiding sign, swept by bitter wind and driving snow. The missionary was for striking straight across the open, but Thomas after the Indian habit was for the more cautious plan of skirting the shore. "De win', she no so bad, and de trail he's no get los'." Paul was for the shore line too.

They had not run for more than half an hour longer when old Skookum, who was leading, began to show signs of anxiety, sniffing, whimpering and uttering short yelps. The missionary pulled up his team short.

"Something coming, sure thing, man or beast," he shouted to the others following. They all stood listening intently, but only the howling and hissing of the storm came to their ears. The dogs had all caught Skookum's restlessness, sniffing and whimpering.

"Huh! Something! Indian think," grunted Thomas, sniffing like the dogs.

"Indian, eh?" said the missionary sharply. "By Jove, it couldn't be——" he paused, looking at Paul.

Quickly the boy's hands went to his lips, he threw back his head and flung out into the storm a long weird call. Thomas glanced quickly at him. "Chippewayan," he grunted.

Faintly and as if from a long way to the lake side came a similar call.

"Peter!" exclaimed Paul, setting off in the direction of the call. The missionary caught and held him fast.

"Hold on! Let's be sure! Call again."

Once more, Paul with his hands to mouth uttered his call and again from the lake came the faint response.

"From there, eh?" said the missionary, pointing north-west.

"*Oui!*" said Thomas, pointing a little farther north. "Indian there!"

But already the boy was off into the blinding drift.

"Hold up, you young fool! We must keep together," cried the missionary, dashing after him. "Follow up, Thomas, with the dogs," he shouted.

Not a sign of the boy could he get, but keeping the line of direction carefully he ran with all his speed, listening intently as he ran. Again there came on the storm wind the long weird call.

"More to the left," he muttered, swinging off in that direction, but keeping up his pace. A few minutes of hard running, and through a break in the drifting storm he caught a glimpse of a huddled group of snow-sheeted spectral figures, and in the midst of them Paul holding in his arms a woman, tall and swaying in the storm like a wind-blown sapling. Clinging to the young man was a child, a little girl, and near by a boy stood, sturdily independent. Instantly the missionary took command.

"Here, Thomas!" he shouted, starting back on his tracks. Soon he met the Indian with the two dog teams, coming along at a gallop. "We have them here, Thomas. Let us make camp at the big headland. Quick! Quick!" Round the little group the Indian swung the teams.

"Get her on to the toboggan, Paul," ordered the missionary. "We camp at the headland. Good shelter and good wood. Only hurry, for God's sake, and follow me."

The woman sank without a word onto one of the toboggans, the little girl upon the other, the boy scorning to ride. And rescued and rescuers made for camp.

Dazed, stupid, devoid of sensation or emotion, Paul trolled after the last toboggan, but through his head the words kept time to his feet: "He maketh the clouds His chariot; He rideth upon the wings of the wind." And he knew that they were true.

CHAPTER XVII

Chief Factor MacKinroy himself would have been the first to assign to the missionary, the Rev. John Chambers, M.A., Oxon., the position of premier influence and even of authority, not only in the little community at the Post but in the whole district tributary to the Post, with its nondescript population of white traders and trappers, half-breeds and Indians. And this was due to those mysterious qualities that go to the making of personality, and to the services which the possession of these qualities fitted him to render. He was the titular head of the Anglican Mission, which of course gave him a standing at once influential and authoritative, but had he not been more his official position as a dignitary of a great church would have gone but a small way to win him place and power.

Fifteen years ago, raw from the greatest university in the English speaking world, he had come up with a Hudson's Bay Company brigade and had planted himself here in this far north outpost of civilisation, to establish a mission in partibus infidelium for his church. Quite a year before his arrival, his coming had been duly announced by the company authorities in London to Factor MacKinroy, who received the announcement with explosive profanity in the "twa langiges" and then speedily forgot all about the thing.

"And who the deevil will you be?" was the Factor's greeting, when the fly-bitten and sorely battered representative of the church disentangled himself from the motley crew of the brigade and presented himself to the Factor's gaze.

"Ah—I beg your pardon. Ah—Chambers is my name——"

"And what the deevil will be your business in these parts ?" inquired the Factor, on the lookout for doubtful characters, rival traders, prying politicians, globe trotters and the like.

"Before I answer your polite inquiry, sir, may I ask who the devil are you ?"

For quite ten portentous seconds the Factor glared at the little man whose steady blue eyes twinkled pleasantly at him out of a face brick red and horribly distorted by the assiduous attentions of the swarms of various kinds of flies, big and little, black, brown and grey, for the past six weeks. During those portentous ten seconds the Factor's keen eyes had been taking stock of the little man before him, with swift appraising glances.

"God bless my soul!" said he at length. "And it is yourself will be the new minister. And I will be asking your pardon, for I can well see you are a man as well."

So began a friendship that fifteen years of mutual knowledge and of common experience of the toils and perils of the wild North land welded into something that no earthly strain could break.

To John Chambers the wild, rude life brought never an hour of regret, never but one. That was the hour after the letter had gone south by the monthly mail, in which he had set free from her engagement the English girl with whom in earlier days and in happier surroundings he had planned his life. But the desperate loneliness was wiped clean from his memory by another hour of ecstatic and delirious joy which followed the incoming of the English mail some three months later. For that mail brought him a letter palpitating with indignant scorn of him and his high-flown and altogether idiotic purpose of self-immola-tion. "What about me, you silly boy?" inquired the writer. "Are you the only person in the world? Now be it known unto you that on or about the thirty-first of March—for I believe your execrable roads break up in the later spring, and I cannot and will not brook delay—

there will be in Edmonton a young female person," here followed a description which the reader of the letter refused to recognise, "looking for convoy and a convoyer to the wild North land. If the convoyer happen to be a little man—you know you are only five feet, eight and three-quarters inches though you protest five feet nine—red headed and much freckled of face and with dear, bold, blue eyes, so much the better," at the reading of which the said convoyer flung the letter high, kicked over his stool, seized his stolid and loyal Indian factotum, Thomas by name, and whirled him into a mad Kai-yai! Hai-yai! war dance.

Together for more than a dozen years they fought the good fight against ignorance, dirt, disease and all the other varieties of humanity's ills in which "the world, the flesh and the devil" manifest themselves and with varying success winning with other rewards the trust, the reverence, the love of Indian, half-breed and white man alike and awakening in all whose love they won the more or less persistent desire to emulate their deeds and attain their likeness, a truly notable achievement.

The rescue of the Indian woman and her family was to the missionary a bit of his ordinary day's work, as was the daily ministering to the sick woman, without questioning and without suspicion, such help for body and soul as she required. The woman's need was great, and for these good Samaritans this established a sufficient claim upon the full wealth of their resources, with never a suggestion or sense of burden. Indeed, within the missionary's home the coming of the little blind girl was as the visit of an angel unawares. It added not a little to the cares of the missionary's wife that she was not infrequently called upon to settle furious strife between her sturdy young sons as to their rights and privileges in the service of the little maid. Within a week the whole family had made for themselves an assured place in the little community about the Post. The only cloud upon the horizon of their community life was the only too obvious fact that the Indian woman was travelling her last trail and that the camp ground was in sight.

Upon this shadowed area of peace came breezing from the south Sergeant Starr on his way to the far north, seeking a runaway half-breed murderer and thief. A cheery soul was the sergeant, in spite of his seventy-three inches of gaunt and grim manhood. He had left his corporal a hundred miles back, nursing, at another Hudson's Bay Company's Post, a frozen foot.

"Where has your man gone, Sergeant?" inquired the factor. "Have you any idea now?"

"Up the Athabasca—among the Chippewayans, I rather guess," replied the sergeant, "and they are the very deuce too to work with. Close as clams. No use for us."

"But you will be getting him in time, I suppose," said the factor dubiously.

"It's a habit we have," said the sergeant, as if gravely announcing a demonstrated fact. "What's new? Who is the young Apollo?" he added, nodding in the direction of Paul who was passing.

"Yon lad is one of a party rescued by Chambers from the teeth of the last blizzard, a week or so ago."

"Chambers is at his old tricks, eh?"

"Aye. And this time he made a very fine catch whatever. Four of them, one a woman, an Indian with a blind little child——"

"What?" exclaimed Starr, arrested in his unloading operations. "A blind girl? An Indian?"

"Half-breed Scotch. Indian mother."

"What name?" enquired the sergeant sharply.

"Name? That I do not know. We don't bother with the names of our guests much," said the factor.

The sergeant nodded. "Quite right, quite right, Mr. MacKinroy. But I am interested in this family. Fine young fellow that. And blind child, eh?"

"And what will you be after, Sergeant?" asked the factor, knowing his man.

"Not much, except that I may say to you, Mr. Mac-

Kinroy, that I am of the opinion that I have hit upon something that the commissioner has been asking us to dig up for the past six years." The sergeant's deliberate voice and manner were quite impressive.

"And what will you be meaning now, Sergeant?"

"Six years ago a family corresponding in numbers and personnel to your rescued party disappeared from the Windermere Valley, vanished into space, absolutely into thin air—quite unbelievable, but actually did, you know. Head's all terribly up in the air about it. Reputation of force and all that, you know. Of course, they had a week's start. Fellow refused to lay information."

"Now then, Sergeant, if you will tell me what you are discoursing upon I will be obliged, but if not you may as well shut your gab," said MacKinroy, athirst for news from the outside and annoyed at the sergeant's scrappy and wholly unsatisfactory account of what offered mystery.

"Oh, I beg pardon, MacKinroy. Forgot you were out of it. The bones of it I'll give you. Chap, Gaspard by name, rancher, artist, tangled up with Indian girl—Athabascan chief's daughter—after his wife died went dippy, married Indian girl, brought her back to ranch with two children, both his, youngest blind girl—my clue, see?—neighbour rancher, Sleeman by name, bad lot, hanging round, monkeying round with Indian woman, Gaspard and his son, this young fellow here I fancy, came on the scene, found her fighting off Sleeman, jumped for his gun, the woman grabbed him to prevent murder, in the struggle Gaspard was shot, died; woman goes quite mad, moons round giving out signs of dementia, one night Sleeman's house goes up in smoke, Sleeman himself pulled out of the fire by one of ours with an ugly knife wound in the ribs, at first charged Indian woman with crime, later refused to make any formal deposition; same night woman and whole bunch vamoose utterly, fade off the landscape, trail lost completely. Of course, every Indian in the North Country sets himself to mix that my people. He tried to do me wrong in his house. I struck him with my knife. The Chippewayan strikes but once. Then I was afraid. I put fire to the house, that my trail might not be found, and, like the storm wind, my pony carried me home. Before we could go Paul found us and came with us. He would not let us go alone. It was folly. Now I have brought him back before the light goes out of my sky. For these long, long years we have been like the wild deer, or the fox in the forests and mountains." She paused, exhausted.

"Yes," said the sergeant, "we could find no trace of you."

"My father's people would leave no trail of the daughter of their chief," she said proudly. "Now," she continued, after she had rested a few minutes, "I bring the son of my man back to his people. He is not Indian, and he must not join himself to my people. I have kept him clean. He will be great among his own people. This his father would wish. I have brought him back. You will take him to his people." She turned her eyes upon the sergeant, waiting his answer.

"I will bring him back," he said. "I give you my word."

"Good! That is all. My work is done now," she said with a little sigh. "I have spoken true words." Once more she kissed the crucifix.

"Listen," said the sergeant. "The man you struck did not die. One of our men pulled him from the burning house. He lives today."

"Sleeman is alive?" exclaimed Paul.

"Alive?" said the Indian woman. "Wait, Paul. You will let me speak." She lay for some moments with eyes closed, then in a voice which shook with emotion she cried, "Alive? Ah! ah! I *was* glad he was dead, now I am glad he is alive. The good Father told me it was not good to go—to pass—with blood on the hands. The Holy Mother was praying for me! It is good!" She turned her dark eyes upon Paul. "No, Paul. You remember your word to your father. That is done." She put her hand on his arm. "No! no! That is not the way of your people. For me? Perhaps. For you? No! It is not your law." Again her eyes searched his pale set face.

"He would have wronged you, Onawata, my father's wife. There is only one thing for me—only one."

"Paul, I have brought you back to your people. I have kept you clean. You will be a great man among your people. You will promise me." She raised herself on her arm. "I go—perhaps I shall see your father, my chief. I cannot go without your word. A-a-ah!" her voice rose in a wailing cry. "To him, to you, I brought only sorrow and shame. Lay on me no more, Paul. I have suffered much." She fumbled under the pillow and drew out and unwrapped a small parcel, carefully wrapped in deer skin. "Take it, Paul. It is your mother's good book. You will kiss it and say you will not kill the man —for her, for her, Paul!" Her voice rose in a cry, her hands reached trembling toward him.

The boy was terribly shaken with the struggle going on in his soul. He knew the book well. He took and turned it over in his hands, opened it at the fly-leaf, read in faded lettering the words written, he well remembered when, "For my son Paul, from his mother. 'Blessed are the pure in heart, for they shall see God.'" The scene flooded his memory—the Pine Croft living room, his mother's face with its wondering, tremulous smile as he told her how up through the tops of the pines, between the little white clouds he could see God looking down at him. He remembered how, as she was tucking him in that night, she brought him a new Bible, with his name in it and her name and the beautiful words about seeing God, and how she kissed the book and kissed him as she gave it into his hands. Like a mountain torrent sweeping away a dam, the surging tide of his emotion swept away his control. He dropped on his knees by the bed, pressed the words to his lips, sobbing.

"Oh, Mother, Mother! dear, dear Mother! For your sake! Yes, yes! for your sake!"

The men turned away and moved softly from the hut, leaving the two alone. The Indian woman lay back, spent and done. She had fulfilled her trust. She had brought back to his people, clean from lust and from blood, the son of the man who was to her as God Himself. Next day the sergeant went north on his quest, carrying a message to the Athabascan chief from his daughter.

The passing of Onawata was all peace. An hour with the missionary, even though he was not of her faith, brought her something of the peace that passeth understanding. There was still her anxiety for the future of her children, which she had settled in her own way. There only remained the telling of it to them, and that she deferred till the very last.

They were together in the little hut after a day of quiet rest and freedom from pain.

"Here, Tanna," she called in her soft Chippewayan tongue. "Come hither, little Singing Water, light of my eyes. Come in beside. me." She gathered the child in her arms and held her close. "Peter, come too." The boy came and knelt by her bed, his dark face set as if cast in bronze. He well knew what was before them all. His mother's arm went round his shoulders.

"Little ones, your mother is going away," she began, her voice coming softly and evenly, like the flowing of quietly running water, "away to a good country—ah! a good country!—where the warm sun is always shining, no frost, no snow, no hunger, no pain, no sickness, no fear, no fighting, no blood. Oh, it is a good country." She lay quiet a few moments, her dark face growing young and beautiful. The little girl's fingers crept over her face.

"Oh, Mammy, you are smiling. When will we go? I do not love the cold and the hunger, and I want no more pain for you, Mammy dear." The little one spoke in her father's tongue. Her mother had seen to that. "And,

Mammy, there will be no more dark. I know! I know!"

The mother drew the little one close to her with a low moaning cry and again she lay silent, drinking slowly to the dregs that last bitter cup that all mothers must drink. But having drunk, she set herself to her last service for them.

"Not today will you come, Singing Water," she said, her voice flowing softly again. "I will go and later you will come, and Peter and Paul. And now you will listen and remember, you and Peter, while the sun shines and the winds blow you will not forget."

"Yes, Mammy," whispered the child.

"You and Peter will go back to my people."

"No," said Paul, speaking with sharp decision. "Where I go they will go."

"They are not your people, Paul."

"They are my father's children."

An eager light came into the woman's eyes.

"Paul! Paul!" she cried in English. "You do not know what you say. They are of my blood. They will be a burden on you. They will spoil your life. Your father, Paul, did not wish that, I know. Peter will be a great chief. He will care for Tanna. I have planned this with my father. They will drag you down as I dragged your father down. I—who would have given him the blood from my heart! You must not do this." Her voice was eager and tremulous with pain. "I will not spoil your life too."

"They are my father's children. They are my brother and sister," said Paul, in a voice steady and strong. "Do you think I can leave Tanna to go back to the blanket and the wigwam? Tanna! my little blind sister!" His voice rang out in indignant scorn. "No, no, Mammy," he added, using Tanna's form of address, rare with him, "say no more. It is settled. They go with me."

A look of great wonder dawned in the woman's eyes— wonder and joy. Raising herself she held out her hands to him.